Maddie tried to s
threatening to engulf her.

She'd seen what they did with her coworker from the hospital. And knew what they'd do to her if they caught her trying to escape.

She quickened her steps across the tangled mass of vines beneath her feet, her rib cage pressing against her lungs as they hurried over a low section of the wall then hurried into the forest. She was terrified they were following in the darkness. Terrified this wasn't really over.

She stumbled, but Grant was there to catch her. She felt his arm wrap around her waist. Felt the warmth of his hands as he steadied her. And caught a glimpse of his expression as he looked at her.

"We're almost there," he said, breaking into her thoughts.

She saw the waiting car as they came out of the thick wooded area. A second later, a streak of orange lit the night air in an arch then dropped back toward the horizon, enveloping the car in a ball of flames.

Lisa Harris is a Christy Award winner and winner of the Best Inspirational Suspense Novel for 2011 from *RT Book Reviews*. She and her family are missionaries in southern Africa. When she's not working she loves hanging out with her family, cooking different ethnic dishes, photography and heading into the African bush on safari. For more information about her books and life in Africa, visit her website at lisaharriswrites.com.

Books by Lisa Harris

Love Inspired Suspense

DESPERATE ESCAPE

LISA HARRIS

HARLEQUIN® LOVE INSPIRED® SUSPENSE

Recycling programs
for this product may
not exist in your area.

LOVE INSPIRED BOOKS

ISBN-13: 978-0-373-44693-3

Desperate Escape

www.Harlequin.com

Printed in U.S.A.

So be strong and courageous!
Do not be afraid and do not panic before them.
For the Lord your God will personally go ahead of you.
He will neither fail you nor abandon you.
—Deuteronomy 31:6

Dedicated to Amber for rooting me on,
helping me keep focused and keeping up with the dishes
as I wrote fervently to not only save Maddie and Grant,
but to also meet my deadline!

ONE

Grant Reese jumped out of the Jeep at the edge of the dirt road behind Antonio, praying his friend's intel was right. Maddie Gilbert's life—as well as their own lives—depended on it. Gray shadows hovered around them like formless figures as they left the car behind and stepped into the thick bush. Already, the last whitish glow of sunlight was preparing to vanish into darkness. There was no dusk here. Just a few moments of shimmering color along the horizon, then nothing but blackness. And even then the vast network of stars hanging across the African night sky wouldn't be able to compete with the extensive canopy of trees that intertwined above them.

"You know this is a suicide mission." Antonio's whisper competed with the hum of insects around them as they forged ahead through the thick undergrowth.

Grant frowned at his friend's comment. Antonio might have agreed to help him, but he'd also made it clear he believed it was foolish to try to rescue Maddie from the middle of an insurgent camp on their own. Grant didn't need anyone to convince him he was about to step into a minefield—both literally and figuratively.

If only a fraction of the rumors he'd heard about this area were true, anyone with half an ounce of intelligence would be running in the opposite direction. Because while it was impossible to tell where the rebels were, he knew they were out there. And if the insurgents didn't get them, one of the dozens of land mines that'd been laid by the local drug traffickers to protect their crops and processing labs very well could.

Yet even those risks didn't outweigh the urgency simmering in his gut to find Maddie. He'd made a promise to her brother and, even with the odds against them, he still had no intentions of breaking it.

"You could wait back at the car," Grant threw out.

"I'm not afraid of dying." Antonio's tone was straightforward. "I'm just making sure you're fully aware of what we're stepping into."

A blade of razor-sharp grass sliced through the back of his calf. Grant reached down to slap at the stinging cut and felt the wet trickle of blood. He'd known the stakes when he signed up to serve his country more than a decade ago. Knew his chances of returning home in a body bag were far higher than average. But he wasn't the one they'd laid in the ground that cold Chicago winter six years ago. Darren had stepped on a land mine they were trying to clear. And nothing he'd done had been able to save his friend.

Grant tried to clear his head of those memories as he stumbled midstride over a rotten log, regained his balance and then continued through the thick undergrowth beside Antonio. "You know I'd rather have you with me, but either way, Maddie's out here somewhere, and I intend to find her."

She'd already been missing for five days, and he

knew that with each hour that passed the probability she was alive decreased. But even that fact hadn't managed to deter him.

"You were always stubborn. I just hope she's worth it," Antonio said. "You and I both know what they'll do to us if we're captured."

Grant slapped at the mosquito buzzing in his ear, knowing exactly what they'd do. And if he didn't die tonight at the hands of those they were trying to stop, he still risked dying from some tropical disease. He laughed inwardly at the irony of the situation as the sun dropped beneath the horizon and darkness quickly closed in on them like a thick wool blanket. No longer able to clearly see the path ahead of him, he slowed his steps and waited for his eyes to adjust to the darkness. Winged insects buzzed around his face, a monkey shrieked in the treetops and something growled in the distance.

He shivered despite the stifling humidity. Maybe he was foolish, but he'd never wavered on his decision when he'd first heard the report that Maddie Gilbert was missing. Never faltered on his resolve to keep his promise to his best friend, who'd died beside him in a combat zone—a death he still blamed on himself.

Three nights ago he'd received a phone call from Frank Gilbert. He was worried sick over his daughter, frustrated with the government red tape and asking for Grant's help. Maddie had been abducted near the hospital where she volunteered, and the body of a coworker had been found nearby. No one knew yet if Maddie was dead or alive, but Grant hoped that her skill as a doctor ended up being the one thing that kept her alive. And that it—along with the prayers of hundreds—would keep her safe until they were able to rescue her.

Within an hour of the phone call, he'd bought his tickets and contacted Antonio, who'd promised to pick him up once he'd arrived. Three planes later—including an eight-hour flight across the Atlantic and a stopover in Dakar, Senegal—he'd arrived at Guinea-Bissau's international airport on Africa's west coast. It was a country most people had never even heard of.

But he knew it well. He'd been a part of a Special Forces military training operation in the region for eighteen months, helping to mentor and instruct local troops intent on curbing drug trafficking. He'd trained new recruits on how to clear the land mines drug traffickers had buried, taught them about the types of mines they would find, offered paramedic courses and further trained section leaders to ensure that the country remained safe.

Antonio had been one of his best students, and to this day was still a close friend. And he had connections. Four hours ago, they'd finally tracked down where Maddie was being held on one of the islands off the mainland. And while they might be on their own, Grant had every intention of bringing her out. Alive.

His mind shifted as they trudged through the thick undergrowth toward the reason he was here. Maddie had been like a younger sister to him, too. She'd always been there at the Gilbert Thanksgiving and Christmas dinners he'd managed to make. And while he'd made an effort to keep in touch with Darren's family, it was mainly Maddie's mom, Alyce, who kept him up-to-date with what was going on with them.

Most of what he knew about Maddie was what her

mother had told him over the years. How she'd excelled through medical school, found a position in a well-established practice and finally met a man she'd planned to marry. The last time he and Alyce had chatted about family she'd told him how Maddie called off her wedding two months before the date, a decision that had surprised everyone. Then she'd joined Doctors International.

A wave of jetlag washed over him. He ran his hand across the back of his neck and wiped away the perspiration. Despite the little sleep he'd gotten over the past few days, he couldn't afford not to be alert. Years of working with explosives had taught him that. All it took was a moment's lapse.

"How much farther until we reach the camp?" he asked.

Antonio pointed to a row of dim lights in the distance and slowed down. "That's the camp, just ahead of us. It's got to be less than a kilometer."

Grant glanced at his friend, knowing exactly what he was thinking. Getting here was the simple part. But now they had to find a way into the camp, rescue Maddie and get out without being caught.

Maddie knew it was dangerous to venture into the compound. But even at the risk of running into one of the armed guards, grabbing a moment of fresh air was worth it. Between the intense smell of chlorine and sewage, the plastered walls of the twelve-by-twelve makeshift infirmary had begun to close in around her.

She hesitated briefly in the doorway of the grass-thatched structure and studied the moonlight filtering through the cracks in the wooden window frame.

Clothes hung on twine strung diagonally in the corner. A small table that held a candlestick pooled with wax. And six thin mattresses on the floor where her new patients lay.

Cholera might be what was trying to snuff out the lives of the rebels, but it was also the one thing saving hers.

She stepped outside and immediately drew in a deep breath of humid air that was tinged with smoke. With the sun now below the horizon, the only sources of light—beyond the moonlight—were the cooking fires, a couple lanterns and a few bare light bulbs strung across the open courtyard bordered by individual sleeping huts.

Men huddled in a small circle around the fire, while a handful of women finished preparing dinner. Above the boisterous conversation was the constant noise of goats and chickens, used to supplement the rebels' diet, and the distant sounds of the forest beyond.

Over the past five days, she'd done everything she knew to contain the unraveling situation, while giving specific instructions how to rid the camp of the disease. She'd taught the women to boil all water used in the camp for drinking and cooking, and gave them all strict instructions on waste management, hygiene and food safety. She even managed to find what she believed to be the origin of the cholera—a contaminated water source less than a kilometer south of the camp. But finding the source was only the beginning of stopping the disease, as more of the men continued to come down with the symptoms.

Without the option of replacing fluids with IVs, she'd opted for a simple homemade oral rehydration recipe using precise measurements of sugar, salt and boiled water, hoping it would be adequate. At least until she could get her hands on some proper medical equipment.

Though containing the epidemic was essential to those in the camp, escape was still in the forefront of her mind. And escape was not going to be easy.

She'd studied the layout of the large compound—individual huts arranged in a circle that surrounded an open space in the middle. Men armed with automatic weapons patrolled the walled perimeter on a rotating basis. Inside the camp, they watched her carefully. The only place they left her completely alone was inside the room they'd given her to treat the sick.

She leaned against the rough bark of a palm tree, thankful for a few moments to refocus her thoughts and pray. Thankful the men were ignoring her for the moment while the women served their spicy yam, onion and tomato stew with rice for dinner.

Her gaze shifted to the walled edges of the camp that were shrouded in darkness. Even if she escaped beyond the compound, that wasn't the only problem she faced. She had no idea where the camp was located, and no way to communicate with the outside world. They'd flown her in and then brought her here blindfolded in an old Jeep. Which was why whatever was out there—beyond the forested edges of the camp—scared her as much as what was inside.

I have no idea what to do, God. No idea how to get out of this alive...

She'd heard stories of Latin America's organized drug runners seeking new routes to Europe via West Africa. Up to two-thirds of the cocaine that moved between the two continents traveled through these small countries, where many of the dealers controlling the trade now lived. The result had been to turn the African coastline into a haven for drug traffickers who could easily afford their safety by recruiting local policemen and paying off government officials.

And now they had her.

She fingered the locket secured around her neck to insure the flash drive was still there. According to journalist Sam Parker, local officials weren't the only ones tapping into the profits. Sam had died with a secret connecting a prominent US State Department employee to this dark world of drug running. As he lay dying in her care from a gunshot wound, he'd whispered to her in ragged breaths how easy it was to organize frequent drug flights, front companies and fake business deals of government officials. The local government claimed it was insurgents involved in trans-Sahara drug trafficking, not their own officials. She had no idea who was telling the truth, but she did know that Sam Parker had died for the information he'd passed on to her.

And if they found out what she knew, she'd be dead as well.

A young girl, Ana, who couldn't be more than ten, stumbled past her lugging a heavy pot of boiled water. Maddie caught her glistening ebony skin in the moonlight.

"Ana?" Maddie reached out to press her hand against the girl's forehead, speaking in Portuguese. "You're burning up."

"I'm fine."

"No, you're not."

Maddie took the heavy pot from her and motioned for her to go inside the room. Cholera wasn't choosy with its victims, but was highest when poverty, war or natural disasters were involved. It only took hours for severe dehydration to set in that, if left untreated, could quickly lead to death. Maddie followed the girl into the stuffy room. Maddie wasn't the only innocent one caught in the crossfire of this drug war. Ana was now infected.

"Lie down, sweetie. We need to get you started on some of the rehydration solution."

She nodded at the one clean bed near the wall and started praying again, wishing she had some antibiotics for her. If given at the beginning, they could shorten the symptoms. But even with all her efforts to disinfect the bedding and dishes, boil all drinking water and monitor the food preparation, the disease was still continuing to spread. Before she'd arrived, three of the men had died from dehydration and renal failure. The ones she was treating now slept in between treatments, still too weak to even sit up.

And it was possible this wasn't the epicenter of the disease. She'd watched the coming and going of the men. If this camp was affected, more than likely so were any nearby towns and villages.

Maddie gave Ana one of the last doses of pain medicine she had, hoping it would bring down the girl's fever, and began asking questions to verify her symptoms. Fever, chills, headache and fatigue, but no diarrhea.

The symptoms didn't match up.

"I don't think you have cholera, but I'm still going to give you some of the rehydration mix. Drink as much of this as you can."

Ana took a sip. "If I don't have cholera, then what is it?"

"I don't have a way to test you, but it's a good chance it's malaria."

Cholera had a way of spreading quickly through a community, but malaria killed hundreds of thousands of people every year, most of them in sub-Saharan Africa. And Maddie had no drugs to fight the parasite. All she could do was monitor Ana closely, make sure she stayed hydrated and try to keep the fever down.

"How long have you lived here?" Maddie asked, taking the opportunity she'd been hoping for to talk to Ana away from the listening ears of her captors.

She shrugged; wide chocolate-colored eyes looked up at Maddie in the flickering light. "As long as I can remember. My mother married one of the men in the camp."

"Where is she now?"

"She died a year ago giving birth."

Maddie caught the sadness in her expression. "And your father?"

"He's dead, too."

"So now you cook and do their laundry."

Ana nodded.

But Maddie knew one day soon the men would start coming to her asking for more than just clean clothes.

"What about school?" she asked, taking the empty cup.

"I liked school, but now…there is too much work to be done."

"Don't you have any other family? Someone else you could live with away from the camp?"

"Before she died, my mother told me I should find a way to get to the capital where my grandmother stays. She lives upstairs in a blue-painted house that has a balcony on a narrow street." A slight smile settled on her lips. "But the mainland is far, and I have no way to get there."

Maddie turned to pour some more of the rehydration drink into Ana's cup and stopped. A figure stood in the darkened doorway. She felt the hairs on the back of her neck stand up.

God, I need You to intervene in this situation... Again...

"I told you it wasn't safe for anyone other than patients to be in here," she said as she stood up to face the man.

The man took another step forward.

"Stop—"

"Wait. It's okay." He continued speaking in perfect English from the shadows, his voice barely above a whisper. "It's Grant Reese."

"Grant? I don't..." She paused midsentence, as memories of a girlhood crush flickered through her mind. How was it possible he was here?

But there was no time to figure out how he'd found her halfway around the world.

A second man stepped in behind him.

"This is my friend Antonio. We need to get you out of here. Now."

"Wait... I can't go." Her mind spun, still unable to determine if this was a dream, or if someone had actually come to rescue her. "Not yet."

"Why?"

"There's a young girl here... Ana..." Like herself, Ana wasn't here by choice. And she wasn't going to leave her behind. "If I leave her here..."

She tried to hold back the fear starting to crush her.

Over the past five days she'd dreamed of some handsome Special Ops soldier coming to her rescue. In her dreams everything might have ended happily ever after, but there was only one ending for this scenario if they tried to escape and got caught. And, she realized, only one ending for Ana if she was left behind.

"Where is she?" Grant whispered.

"Right here with me." Maddie turned to Ana. "Do you want to leave with us?"

"Yes—"

"I'm not sure that's possible," Antonio interrupted.

"We have to take her," Maddie said, pulling a thin blanket around the girl's neck and grabbing the backpack she'd had on her when she'd been abducted. She had so many questions, but all of them would have to wait for now. "And we need to hurry. The guards are eating and won't be paying a lot of attention for the next few minutes, but they'll be done soon. How far do we have to walk?"

She tightened her grip around Ana's waist. There was no way the girl could walk out of here on her own.

"Just over a kilometer," Grant said. "We've got a car waiting. Then we'll drive to the airstrip where we have a plane ready to pick us up."

"I'll carry her," Antonio said, reaching down to pick her up.

Maddie nodded and turned back to Grant, wishing she could see the familiar bright blue eyes she remembered all too well. "Thank you. Both of you."

"You can thank us later, once we get out of here in one piece," Grant said.

She slipped through the shadows behind them toward the edge of the compound, trying to swallow the fear threatening to engulf her. Because she'd seen what they had done with her coworker from the hospital. And knew what they'd do to her if they caught her trying to escape.

She glanced back at the cooking fires, before hurrying to catch up with Grant. The men were still busy eating, and there were no signs of any of the guards in front of them. But even that didn't help calm the panic. She quickened her steps across the tangled mass of vines beneath her feet, her rib cage pressing against her lungs as they hurried over a low section of the wall and then hastened into the forest. She was terrified the men were following in the darkness. Terrified this wasn't really over. Because somehow, she'd become the prey in a game she didn't know how to play.

She stumbled, but Grant was there to catch her. She felt his arm wrap around her waist. Felt the warmth of his hands as he steadied her. And caught a glimpse of his expression as he looked at her.

"We're almost there," he said, breaking into her thoughts.

She caught a glimpse of the waiting car as they came out of the thick wooded area. A second later, a streak of orange lit the night air in an arch and then dropped back toward the horizon, enveloping the car in a ball of flames.

TWO

Maddie watched in horror as flames completely consumed the vehicle. She stumbled backward, away from the heat radiating from the car. Someone had to have seen them escape, which meant they needed to run. But where? Darkness had long since settled in around them. Without a vehicle—without knowing where they were going—finding their way out of here was going to be almost impossible.

And whoever had set off the explosion was somewhere nearby. She searched beyond the blaze lighting up the night sky, but saw no one.

Please, God, please... You've brought us this far. There has to be another way out.

"What do we do now?" she asked.

"We run!" Grant grabbed Maddie's hand as she continued to pray, pulling her away from the scene with Antonio carrying Ana right behind them.

Smoke filled her lungs as they ran. Her eyes burned, and her legs threatened to give out, partly from fear, partly from the excursion. Her mind scrambled to sort through the facts as she knew them, while trying not to stumble beside Grant. She'd seen the explosion. Someone had purposely blown up that car. Which meant they were out there. After them. Guilt slivered through her. Grant should never have tried to come after her. Even with his military background, he'd put not only his life, but the life of Antonio at risk. And she'd seen the kind of men who had been holding her. Even if they ran, they would come after them.

Lit only by the night sky, Maddie clutched the strap of her backpack with one arm and struggled to keep up with Grant as they ran along a narrow dirt path, shielded on one side by the thick forest. She glanced back, worried about how long Antonio would be able to carry Ana. Worried about how long all of them could continue at this pace. All she could do was pray that the shadows would play to their advantage and hide them from the rebels.

Grant's hand gripped hers as they ran. Silvery traces of moonlight encircled them, bathing the surrounding terrain in a hazy glow. How had her situation escalated to this? Until the past few days, she'd firmly believed her decision to come to Africa had been worth any inconveniences of life in a foreign country. Even if her decision to come had been partly selfish.

After four years of dating "Mr. Right," reality had hit her, and she'd realized she was about to make the biggest mistake of her life in settling for what everyone else wanted for her. But not what was best for her. In joining a medical team working in Guinea-Bissau and escaping the American rat race, she'd hoped to find a missing part of herself in helping others.

What she'd found had been far more than she'd expected.

While her family had been convinced she was crazy

for even considering the idea, it had been here, in one of the poorest countries in the world, that she'd found an unexplainable joy. And slowly, she'd begun to find that missing piece of herself. Even the tragedy and heartache she faced at the hospital every day was countered by the deep sense of community, faith and a life never taken for granted by those around her.

She kept running. The sticky night air pressed against her and her lungs. She fought for air as she listened for signs of pursuit from behind. Lightning struck in the distance. The night around them hummed with the sounds of insects and other nocturnal creatures. If someone was after them, she couldn't hear them.

Grant held up his hand and then led her off the road and into the edges of the dark forest. "We'll stop here for a moment. Hopefully we've put enough distance between us and whoever's out there, but I need to contact my pilot. Keep your eyes out for anyone following us."

Grant pulled out a phone from his back pocket. Maddie pressed her hand against her chest, trying to catch her breath while he held up his phone to get a better signal. Lungs still constricted, she bent down next to Ana where Antonio had laid her on the ground. The young girl groaned, but at least her fever was down slightly.

"I can't get through," Grant said, walking another dozen feet away from them, still holding up the phone.

Antonio knelt down beside her. "How is she?"

"I'm pretty sure it's malaria, but I don't have the resources to treat her properly. I can give her the rehydration drink for now, but she needs to be at a proper hospital with an IV drip and a dose of antimalarial drugs."

For now—just like at the camp—she'd have to do with their limited resources.

Maddie looked up as Grant walked back toward them. Memories flooded through her mind. He had always been the tall, quiet hero she'd looked up to. Her brother's best friend. The man who brought toffee for the holidays and refrigerator magnets from his travels for her mom. He'd also been the man who'd cried at Darren's funeral and stood beside her as they laid the casket into the ground.

And now he'd come to rescue her.

"Why'd you come for me?" she asked. She caught the weight of the situation in his gaze.

He hesitated as he studied her face. "I promised your brother before he died I'd look after you."

And six years later he'd risked his life to keep that promise?

Her heart stirred as she dropped her gaze. "What do we do now?"

"I sent a text to the pilot. All I can do now is hope it gets through. I'm worried he might be walking into a trap if they land at the airstrip right now."

"Who is he? Your pilot friend."

"His name's Colton Landry. He dropped us here three hours ago. He grew up on both sides of the border. His mother's from Michigan and his father's French Canadian. He works as a pilot for West African Mission Aviation. They use aircraft to help provide medical care, rescue and disaster relief, as well as transport of medical and food supplies."

"And he agreed to be a part of your crazy plan?"

He shot her a smile. "You needed to be rescued."

Maddie looked away to search the black night for movement but saw nothing. Except for thunder rumbling in the distance, an eerie quiet greeted her. With limited options she had no idea what the next-best move was. She'd heard the planes take off and land from the small, nearby airfield and realized the strip must be a part of the drug route. Which meant Grant could be right. If someone knew they were coming, then more than likely they'd be watching the airstrip.

She'd seen what they'd done to the vehicle. They could easily do the same thing to the plane.

Grant turned to Antonio. "What do you think? You know this area better than any of us. What's the best way out of here?"

"The only other way off this island is by boat."

Maddie knew that finding their way in the dark was going to be difficult, if not impossible. And extremely dangerous.

"How far to the port?" Grant asked.

Antonio glanced at Ana. "Without a vehicle…at night…"

"There's a couple of Jeeps back at the camp," Maddie said. "If we go back—"

"It's not worth the risk going back," Antonio said. "We got lucky one time. A second time…"

"He's right," Grant said.

"Then what?" Maddie asked. "We can't go back, we can't continue? Is that what you're saying? And what if they come after us?"

"I don't think it's a question of if, but when." Grant slid his phone into his back pocket.

Antonio knelt down and started drawing a crude map of the area with a stick. "Our options are limited without a plane. Drug traffickers use these islands for a reason. Not only because they're fairly isolated, but our police force doesn't own a boat, so they're pretty much free to do what they want."

Once Maddie had made the decision to come to Africa, she'd studied everything she could find on the tiny West African country of Guinea-Bissau. About half the size of South Carolina, it included dozens of isolated islands off its coast. Even on the mainland, there wasn't a developed or well-maintained infrastructure, and on top of that only around 10 percent of the roads were paved. Which was the primary reason the majority of the population lived within a dozen miles of a waterway.

But, like Antonio had implied, she also knew that the lack of an easy way out wasn't the only issue they were facing. The country—its islands in particular—had become a drug trafficker's dream. Drugs arrived from South America and were temporarily stored in warehouses, where wholesalers turned around and quickly transported them out of the country—on speedboats along the coast, by overland routes and even by swallowers who ingested the capsules and left via commercial flights to their final destination in Europe.

"So our best way out?" Grant asked.

"We're here," Antonio explained, pointing to his map. "On one of the dozens of islands off the coast, and we need to get to the mainland. Our best chance is to head away from here on foot toward the sea, where we can eventually catch a boat to the mainland."

Grant nodded and moved to pick up Ana. "We need to get going. I'll carry her for a while."

A hundred yards farther, Maddie heard a rustling in the woods beside them. Her heart threatened to explode. Six armed men stepped out of the darkness, and surrounded them.

Grant slowly lowered Ana to the ground and stepped in front of the armed men, hoping to keep her and Maddie out of the line of fire. Maybe his cockeyed plan to rescue her had been too risky, but no matter what happened in the next few minutes, he still didn't regret his decision to come. Waiting for official channels to move could have easily taken weeks, even months. And more than likely, they would have killed her before that happened.

He glanced at Maddie and caught the determined tilt of her chin. Good. She was going to need every ounce of fight she could muster. Because this wasn't over. Not yet. If he had anything to do with it, they were still going to find a way out of here.

"They're taking us back to the camp," Antonio said, translating for the leader who spoke one of the local dialects.

"Wait…" Grant took a step forward and nodded at Antonio. "Ask them what they want?"

As far as the intel he'd gathered, they'd never said why they'd taken Maddie in the first place. There had been no ransom demands, and, in fact, no communication at all. It had only been because of Antonio and his contacts on the island that they'd been able to discover where she was being held in the first place. But his gut told him if they stepped back into that camp a second time, the chances of them coming out alive would greatly diminish. And money was the only bargaining chip he had at the moment.

He waited while Antonio spoke with them. He knew the reasoning behind not paying ransoms. Instead of freedom, it gave terrorists both publicity and cash. And ransom payment led to future kidnapping and, in turn, additional ransom payments. But that was all theoretical and easy to defend when you weren't the one standing in the middle of nowhere with a gun pointed at your head.

"They said you'll have to speak with Oumar back at the camp. He's the one in charge," Antonio said, his jaw tensed.

A radio crackled, and one of the men started talking as they motioned them into the forested inlet. Grant picked up Ana and hurried beside Maddie as they headed back toward the camp. Prayers that he normally struggled finding the words for suddenly flowed.

We're in over our heads, God. And I'm the one responsible to get Maddie—to get all of them—out of here alive. I'm running out of options and to be honest could use some help.

He glanced at Maddie as they followed the men deeper into the woods. Asking for help, from anyone, had always been hard for him. Maybe that had been his problem all along. With his parents. With Darren...

The voice on the other end of their captor's radio shouted, the words distorted. Urgent. Grant glanced at Antonio, wishing they were speaking in Portuguese so he could understand what had happened.

"Rapido!" One of the men hit Grant against the back of his legs with the butt of his rifle. "Hurry!"

"What's going on?" Grant asked.

"I don't know," Antonio said. "There's been some kind of accident."

Grant calculated their odds of escaping as they started back through the forest. White light from a flashlight created shadows among the trees. There was no way they were going to be able to overpower six armed men. They'd have to follow orders. For now.

Grant glanced at Maddie and caught the fear in her eyes. And he didn't blame her. Every time he'd walked out to clear a minefield, a part of him had known he could be taking his last step. But she was used to preventing death as a doctor. Not facing it head-on.

Five minutes later they were back at the camp. Someone shouted. Several of the men ran toward them carrying a body across the courtyard. One of the petrol lanterns caught the face of the young boy. He couldn't be much older than ten or eleven, ebony skin, full lips, dark eyes...

It was the eyes that stopped Grant cold.

The boy's gaze ripped through him. He could read the pain and panic on his face, but there was something more. Something in his eyes that seared through Grant, as if the boy knew that what happened in the next few frightful moments would determine whether or not he would live or die. Because he'd seen that same look before. He'd seen it in Darren's gaze the day he'd died.

Nightmare images he'd tried to erase flashed in front of him. While they'd known the dangers of their job, a small part of them had always held on to the belief that they were invincible. Because if they'd let themselves believe death was going to win, they'd never have stepped out into those fields.

But they'd been wrong.

One miscalculated move had killed his best friend.

Grant set Ana down on a mat as the men laid the boy on a table and shouted at Maddie. He forced himself to take a second look, because the boy's haunted countenance wasn't the only thing that had left his heart racing. Blood soaked through a cloth wrapped around his thigh. The boy's leg—from his knee down—was gone.

He was in Afghanistan again. He could still see the flashes of an explosion, hear Darren's screams. His best friend had become one of the statistics. Sixty million mines were still left unexploded in seventy countries… sixty-five people maimed or killed every day…

He forced his mind to focus on what was going on.

"Get me some more light," Maddie shouted as she started cutting off the clothing around the wound.

"What can I do?" Grant asked.

"We need to get the wound cleaned and covered. There's clean, boiled water, covered in pots behind you." Her hands shook as she turned to one of the men. "I'll do everything I can to save your son, but I want you to promise to let us go once I get him stabilized."

"You're in no position to bargain, because I'm the only one keeping you alive right now," he said, holding her gaze. "So if my son dies…you will all die."

THREE

Grant held up one of the lanterns in order to give Maddie the light she needed to work. He avoided the boy's panicked gaze, trying unsuccessfully to distance himself emotionally from the situation. His emergency training had taught him the basics of what to do, but the clinical instructions were never the same as experiencing them firsthand.

Especially when it was personal.

"What's his name?" Maddie asked the older man in Portuguese.

"Jose."

"Jose… I'm going to do everything I can to help you, but I need you to stay strong. I need you to say with me."

Memories flashed. With Darren, he and his teammates had done everything they could to save his life. But by the time the helicopter had arrived to evacuate them, too much time had passed. Darren had gone into shock, and it had been too late to save him.

"You need to get him to a hospital." Maddie addressed the father while she worked to control the bleeding with direct pressure. "I can try to stabilize him—for now—but he'll die out here in the bush without proper medical treatment."

The older man's fingers gripped edge of the table where his son lay. "I warned you, and I meant it. If my son dies… I will kill you."

"You're not listening to me." Maddie added another layer of fabric around the wound. "I don't have the antibiotics, let alone the tools to do vascular repairs. And if he makes it, he'll need outpatient and occupational therapy to regain as much function as possible. I can't do any of that here. You've got a plane… It's your *only* way to save his life."

"Oumar…" A woman ran up to where they were working and let out a loud wail when she saw the boy. "Oumar, no…they told me what happened. What have you done to our boy?" She turned to the older man and started beating his chest. "You let this happen to him."

He grabbed her hands, ordering her to stop. "I haven't done anything. He knows better than to go play in the woods."

"You're his mother?" Maddie asked.

"Yes." The woman pulled away from her husband and grabbed the hand of her son, her dark eyes filled with panic.

"He needs to go to a hospital where they have the equipment to treat him. He will die if he stays here."

"Please, Oumar. You must do what she says. She is a doctor."

He stepped away from the table and spat something into the radio before turning back to Maddie. "Then you're coming with me—"

"No." Maddie clenched her jaw. "I'm staying here."

Grant caught the flash of fire in her gaze despite the marked fatigue in her eyes, and knew exactly what she was thinking. Their best chance to stay alive was to stay together.

"No?" The older man aimed his weapon at Maddie. "No? If you don't go with me, then I don't need you anymore. Any of you."

"Wait." Grant grasped Maddie's wrist and stepped in front her. "That's where you're wrong. You have a camp full of sick men, which means you still need her here. Antonio and I have medical training. We can help as well."

The man shook his head. "If I leave her here, you'll help her escape again."

"Oumar, please." Jose's mother grabbed his arm, pleading with him. "There is no time for fighting. Jose will die while you stand here arguing. And your men as well. They're right. You need them here."

Grant felt his lungs expand. He held his breath as they waited for the old man's response. The tension felt as thick as the humidity. His fingers closed tighter around Maddie's wrist until he could feel her heart's rapid pulse. He knew she was scared, but he hadn't flown halfway around the world to fail, nor did he have any intention of breaking his promise to her brother. One way or another, they were going to get her out of here.

"Fine." The old man dropped his hands to his sides, the situation defused for the moment. "I'll leave you here—all of you—alive for now. But I will deal with you when I return."

He watched as the older man began shouting orders to the other men. A makeshift gurney was rigged, and orders were sent to the pilot. Grant turned around to face Maddie, slipping his hand down her wrist until their fingers touched. With his other hand, he reached out and wiped her damp cheek with his thumb.

"Are you going to be okay?" he asked.

"For now." She looked up at him, eyes wide open. "But this epidemic is going to be under control soon. And after that...they won't need us."

He pulled her a few inches closer. "We're going to get out of here."

She nodded, clearly wanting to believe his words as much as he did. "I owe you one. More than one, actually." A smile briefly crossed her lips before she pulled away from him and started washing down the table with disinfectant. "If nothing else, you bought us some time."

He worked beside her to clean up, impressed with the way she'd gained control over the situation. She asked one of the women to make a diluted mixture of cooked cereal and water for the cholera patients she'd been treating, while several of the men headed into the forest with Jose. He realized he'd misjudged her strength. There was no doubt her parents loved her. They spoke of how smart and accomplished she was, but they'd been against her coming here. Believed she was wasting her God-given talents and wouldn't be able to handle the work.

But they'd been wrong.

He'd seen the courage in her eyes. The boldness it had taken to stand up to her captors. Maybe it was true that difficulties brought out hidden strengths in a person, but there was more about Maddie Gilbert than met the eye—something that part of him wanted to stick around and discover even after all of this was over.

But that was something he couldn't afford to do.

She turned to him, breaking the silence that had

fallen between them as they continued working. "You were there when Darren died."

It was a statement rather than a question, but one he'd never spoken of with her. After the funeral, he'd answered her parents' questions about that day, knowing if Maddie ever needed those same answers from him he'd be there to tell her.

"Yes," he nodded. "I was there."

"Did tonight remind you of that day?"

She might not have been there that night, but she had to be facing some of the same haunting images of losing her brother he was.

"Yes. It was…almost as if I was there again, during those final moments."

A place he dreamed about at night. A place he longed to escape.

She scrubbed at an invisible mark on the table. "Two weeks after I arrived here, I had to treat my first land mine victim. All I could see was Darren."

"Somehow we didn't think it could happen to us. We were out to save the world. Invincible. Always wishing we could ignore the fact that all it took was one wrong step…"

She stopped to look up at him, allowing the light from the lantern to catch the yellow-copper colors in her eyes. The soft curve of her lashes. "Thank you," she said.

Grant fought to push away the unexpected draw. "I haven't got you out of here yet. I told your mom I planned to have you back by Christmas, and I'm going to do everything in my power to keep my promise."

"It's hard to believe Christmas is in a couple weeks." A look of sadness registered on her face. "But I'm not just thanking you for today. I'm talking about your being there the night Darren died. *And* for coming to rescue me. You didn't have to come."

He touched her arm briefly before pulling away. "Yes, I did. I owe Darren."

He might not have been able to save his friend, but he *was* going to save Maddie.

"Is that why you came to rescue me?" She asked. "Because of Darren's death?"

His face must have betrayed his thoughts for her to ask such a pointed question.

"No…I…" He didn't know how to answer. He didn't want to answer. Because she was right. He'd come to play hero and make up for not saving Darren. Which meant he hadn't come for noble purposes. Not really. He'd come to ease his own conscience.

Her gaze shifted back to the table and, as if reading his thoughts, she said, "I know what it's like to do something good for the wrong reasons."

"What do you mean?"

"I came here, in a way, because of Darren, too. I was looking for what he found with his career. I hoped that somehow helping others would help me find that missing part of myself."

"And did you?"

She shrugged at the question. "It depends on the day, I suppose. I came here convinced I'd save the world. Instead I've had to realize I can't fix everyone. People are going to die, and I can't stop it."

Like Darren.

"But then," she continued, "there are times where I think I'm making a difference in one person's life and somehow…that's enough."

"Darren was always so proud of you." Grant dropped

the rag he'd been using into the bucket of soapy water they'd been using to clean up. "He talked about you all the time. His little sister studying to become a doctor."

Her smile lit up her face this time. "I like to think he would have been proud of my coming here as well. My parents weren't too happy about my decision, though. I was supposed to marry Ben, join some swanky family practice and spend the rest of my life working nine-to-five and having their grandbabies. And while there's nothing wrong with that, it wasn't enough for me."

He watched her wash her hands and then motion to one of the women to get more boiled water while she grabbed bags of salt and sugar for the rehydration mix.

"Can you hand me those cups?" she asked him. "With no Google available out here, thankfully I have the measurements memorized."

He watched her work, jumping in to assist when she asked. He couldn't help but see the irony in the fact that her skills as a doctor had saved her. And yet as soon as the epidemic was controlled, there was a good chance they would kill her.

"I guess this wasn't what you imagined when you signed up with Doctors International," he said.

"Being kidnapped? Not exactly." She let out a soft laugh as she started mixing up the drink for her patients. "Though the past few months haven't been without challenges, either. Most of the time, I've been working up north, in a small rural hospital. Every day, I see the same thing over and over in the maternity ward. It's stifling inside. There are rusty ceiling fans, but no electricity. In the US, one in just over two thousand women will die giving birth. Here, it's one in less than twenty. Most don't even consider going to a clinic. And even if they do, most—especially those in the rural areas—can't make it to the hospital."

He knew the issues she faced on a daily basis. Diesel generators were the primary source of electricity in the capital, and that lack of infrastructure spread throughout the entire country. There was one functioning hospital and even there equipment was limited. Most of the country's health facilities had no electricity. Generators came to life during surgery, but there wasn't enough fuel to run them continuously for refrigeration to store blood donations or for incubators for babies born too soon.

"But that's not the entire picture," she continued. "I see the smile of the children when I go out into the villages to teach preventative care, and the love the mothers have for their babies. Old men sit on mats outside thatched roofs, playing with their grandchildren, while chickens and goats run around. It's a completely different world than the one I grew up in. But when I sit down and talk to the women about their pregnancy, or the babies they've lost and the children they're trying to provide for, I realize just how similar we really are."

"I've discovered the same thing everywhere I've lived. Most of the differences pale when you start working together to make things better."

"I wish my parents could understand that. I've tried to share with them why I needed to come…and why I still want to be here." She stopped and looked up at him. "But I haven't asked you about them, because I know they can't be taking this well. Do you think they're going to be okay?"

Her unspoken question hovered between them.

Were they going to be okay if she didn't make it home alive?

"They're scared," he said. "They will do anything to get you back. Because they've already lost one son, and they don't want to lose you as well."

She nodded. "I watched their reaction to losing Darren. I never meant to put them through something like that again."

"You're not going to, because we're going to find a way out of this."

He watched her continue to work, realizing that she was different from most of the women he knew. Most were happy with the dream of a white picket fence and a husband. Problem was, he'd never be able to give someone those things. And so far had never found anyone who was willing to break that mold with him. Maddie, though, was clearly different.

Maybe when all of this was over…when life went back to as close to normal as possible, he'd consider finding a way to get to know his best friend's little sister…

She glanced at a couple of the armed guards as they walked by. "As soon as we're done here, I need to talk to you about something. Privately."

"About?" Her statement brought him back to reality.

Her hand moved to the locket hanging around her neck. "Information connected to what's going on here."

An hour later, Maddie walked toward the fire, fighting the exhaustion coursing through her body. Her head throbbed and her legs felt like jelly. But it wasn't just the physical fatigue she was dealing with. The emotional strain of the past few days was taking its toll.

She'd finished making up the rehydration mix and checked on each of the patients she'd been treating. While antibiotics would have shortened the duration of the symptoms, ensuring each person was rehydrated was what mattered most. "Are you done?" he asked.

"For the moment." She tugged on the end of her ponytail as she sat down beside him on the fallen tree stump being used as a bench. She'd always seen him as a hero, saving the world alongside her brother. And now, all these years later, that was exactly what he was. The hero who'd flown all the way across the Atlantic to save her. While keeping his promise to her brother.

She caught his profile in the firelight and felt a flurry of emotion pass through her that she didn't know how to identify. She'd always seen him as strong and capable of anything, with those bright blue eyes and a hint of stubble across his chin. She'd also known firsthand the risks he took every day to save the lives of others.

What she couldn't remember was having more than a handful of one-on-one conversations with him over the years. And those talks had always been more awkward exchanges, at least for her, because she'd had a crush on him and hadn't wanted anyone to know. Especially Grant or her brother. Darren had always seen her as the little sister he had to keep safe from the world. Even when she'd been all grown up and in medical school. And she'd always imagined Grant saw her in the same way. So she'd made herself forget about him. Until today.

"Are you hungry?"

She looked up at Grant's question, realizing one of the women was standing in front of her with dinner.

"I'm sorry."

The woman handed her a bowl of stew. She thanked her, but her appetite had long since vanished. She tried to eat a few bites, but only to keep up her strength.

"How's Ana?" Antonio asked from the other side of Grant.

"I'll have to watch her carefully, but the rehydration drink already seems to be helping and her fever's gone down some."

"That's good news," Grant said.

"Yes, it is. I just wish I could treat her properly."

Grant pulled out a zippered canvas tote from the backpack he'd been carrying. "One of the men confiscated most of what I brought, including the two-way radios and phones, but I convinced them to let me keep the clothes your mother sent. Your parents met me at the Denver airport before I flew out. She thought you might need a few things when I found you."

When he found her. Not if.

Maddie felt a surge of emotion as she looked down at the set of blue scrub pants and T-shirt with the Doctors International logo she'd been wearing since they snatched her. Grant's reminder that the holidays were just around the corner had managed to make her feel more homesick.

Even as a med student, when she might've had to come late or leave early, she'd never missed Christmas with her family. Her mother would have already decorated the tree and started planning the meal that would include all of the relatives in a hundred-mile radius as well as a handful of people from church who didn't have family nearby.

She balanced her dinner on her lap and opened the bag her mom had sent. A pair of tan pants, a black tank top and an olive-colored button-down shirt, along with some underwear, a purple sundress, a compact Bible and a small toiletry bag full of travel-size products, including a toothbrush.

"I wish I could have brought more—"

"No. Wow. This is perfect. I never knew how excited I could get over deodorant and a new toothbrush." She let out a soft chuckle and smiled at him. "Thank you. Now all I need is a hot shower."

"There's a letter in there as well from your mother."

She pulled out the pink envelope and traced her finger across her mother's handwriting on the front. She'd wait to read it later when she was alone and didn't have to keep her emotions in check. Because at the moment it wasn't going to take much for her to lose it.

"You said you needed to talk to us about something," Grant said.

She set the bag down beside her and picked back up her bowl of food, keeping her voice low enough to ensure none of the guards across the compound could hear her. "I'm sure you know that this is not just some military camp. The men here are involved in drug trafficking, and their network is extensive."

Antonio nodded. "My country's involvement in the trade is no secret. Cocaine barons of South America use countries like mine as part of their route to dealers in Europe."

For as much as she'd seen, she still had questions. "As a doctor I've heard the rumors, and I've seen firsthand patients who have overdosed from cocaine. But why do they stop here? Why not just fly directly to Europe?"

"It's a way to avoid detection of large shipments by European militaries," Antonio said.

"So, what?" she asked. "They break up their shipment and then transport it?"

"Exactly. It's sent by smaller aircraft or even by human mules. South American cartel members show up here with more firepower than our police and military put together. Our police don't have handcuffs or computers or even enough guns for our officers. They, on the other hand, have money, rifles, ammunition and know every inch of this country's remote areas. They can literally buy the government and do what they want."

"Enough money to pay people off to look the other way and make what they do even easier," Grant said.

"They brought me here because they needed a doctor," she continued. "And I'm sure you know by now that they shot and killed my supervisor, Gavin Richards, when they found out he wasn't a doctor."

She closed her eyes for a moment, wishing she could erase what she'd seen. She'd tried to stop them, but could only watch as one of them pulled the trigger. Simply because they didn't need him.

I need You to help me through this, God...please.

She drew in a slow breath. "But that's not all. The day before I was abducted, I met a man at the hospital during one of my shifts. His name was Sam Parker."

"Sam Parker." Grant leaned forward, his arms resting against his thighs. "He's a journalist, isn't he?"

Maddie pushed her food around on her plate with her spoon, nodded.

"I saw something about him on the news before I left the States," Grant said. "He was shot, wasn't he?"

"Yeah. He was here in the country doing some research for a spread in a magazine and stumbled across a story someone didn't want to get out. Whoever it was tried to kill him. Initially he survived, and a Good Samaritan brought him to the hospital where I treated him for a gunshot wound, but he didn't live through the night."

Maddie hesitated before continuing. Death had always been a part of her job, but lately she'd seen so much tragedy. Tragedies that should never have happened. She leaned forward and lowered her voice, her dinner forgotten. "Before he died, he told me he had evidence of a high-profile US State Department employee tied to this country's drug trafficking."

Grant let out a low whistle. "That's a big story."

"Yes, it is," she said.

"And plausible," Antonio added. "The trans-Atlantic traffickers of drugs and other illegal substances need countries where they can not only fly under the radar of the international community, but also—due to high corruption—not have to worry about the local authorities. And with the profits involved, it's not surprising to discover there are outsiders involved.

"Do you have a name?" he asked.

"No, but I've got something just as good." She clutched the locket she was wearing between her fingers. "It's a flash drive with the evidence Sam was planning to expose. He said if anyone found it he could tell them it was a gift for his girlfriend and no one would think twice."

Grant glanced behind them where a couple of the guards were laughing and drinking. "Does anyone know you have this information?"

"It's possible someone saw me talking with Sam." She shook her head. "But when he gave it to me, there was no one else in the room except for a few sick patients, and I'm sure they weren't paying attention."

"So you think you were kidnapped just because they needed a doctor...not because of the information Sam gave you."

"As far as I know."

"Whatever the reason, we need to get you out of here."

Grant didn't have to say anything else for her to know what he was thinking. Once the epidemic was under control, she'd be disposable—all of them would be—just like Gavin.

"But how do we get out of here?" Maddie asked. "If they're guarding the airstrip and the only other way off this island is by water..."

Grant looked around the camp. "We're looking at a couple dozen armed men who are currently focused more on what they're drinking than us at the moment."

"But if they catch us a second time," Maddie said. "They'll shoot first and ask questions later."

Her stomach knotted. She set down the plate of food beside her, knowing he was right. This was it. There would be no second reprieve.

Someone slipped through the shadows behind them and sat down on the log next to Maddie. Jose's mother. She was carrying an infant tied securely around her back with a piece of wide, colorful cloth. Sliding the baby around in front of her, the mother pulled her out of the makeshift sling and handed the baby to Maddie.

Maddie took the infant and cradled her in her arms.

"I think she might have the sickness." She lowered her voice, her eyes on the guards who sat on the other side of the fire, and added, "You helped save my son. I'm going to help you escape."

FOUR

Maddie's heart rate accelerated.

She was offering to help them escape?

Maddie moved aside a section of the colorful blue-and-orange cloth that was wrapped tightly around the baby, wondering if she'd understood the woman correctly. Because why would she want to help them escape? If Oumar found out, it could cost her her life.

Big brown eyes stared up at her as Maddie pressed the back of her hand against the baby's plump cheeks. She squirmed beneath her touch and cooed at Maddie. No fever. No signs of distress.

"I don't understand…" Maddie paused. She didn't even know the woman's name. "I'm sorry…what is your name?"

"Silvia. And you are Dr. Gilbert." She kept her gaze on Maddie, her voice loud enough to reach the guards. "I need you to make sure she is all right. I cannot lose another child."

"Okay." Maddie glanced at Grant and stood up. The woman obviously needed to talk. "My medical bag is on the other side of the compound. It would be easier if I examined her there."

"Where do you think you're going?" One of the guards set his empty plate of food beside him and walked over to them, grabbing Maddie. She tried to pull away from his grip, but his fingers dug deeper into her arm. "I said where are you going?"

Maddie raised her chin, resisting the urge to say something she'd regret later. "I need to examine her baby."

"You heard Oumar." Grant stood up beside her, ready to step in if needed. "She was brought here to stop this sickness from spreading. And I'm pretty sure that if his child were to die from this disease, he'd want to blame someone."

The guard hesitated.

"Leave her alone." One of the men laughed on the other side of the fire, clutching a bottle of alcohol. "They're not going anywhere."

The guard lessened his grip and let her go before aiming his rifle toward Grant and Antonio. "The two of you will stay here."

Maddie pulled away and walked slowly beside the baby's mother across the courtyard toward her make-shift clinic. She wished the conditions were more ad-equate, and hoped she could do something to put this mother's mind at ease. But even more pressing at the moment was a hope that Silvia might have a way for them to escape.

"I'll be right back. My medical bag's just inside." Maddie handed the baby back to Silvia and pointed to one of two chairs she'd been using to examine pa-tients. She grabbed her bag and sat down across from the woman before pulling out her stethoscope. The only medical supplies she had with her were the ones she'd been carrying the day they'd abducted her; barely more than a handful of painkillers, bandages and antibacterial creams. But at least she had what she needed to assess vital signs and perform a handful of basic emergency procedures.

Maddie picked up the baby in order to examine her again. "Your husband was right to take your son to the capital."

"What happened to him is far too common. They say when the rain falls, the soil shifts. Footpaths that people have used for years suddenly become death traps." Silvia reached up to slip a loose end of her headscarf back into place, her eyes filled with tears. "Do you think he will live?"

Maggie hesitated. Facing one of the lowest life-expectancy rates in the world, death might be all too common in this country, but even that familiarity with loss could never erase the deep anguish these mothers faced. The loss of a child was profound no matter who you were.

"I wish I could say he'll make it, but I can't make any promises. All we can do now is pray."

Silvia's gaze dropped. "Then I hope God listens this time. I've lost three children. I cannot lose the two I have left."

Maddie pressed the stethoscope against the baby's dark brown chest and listened to the steady heartbeat, wishing there was something she could say to ease the woman's pain. But sometimes words weren't enough. "Any diarrhea or vomiting?"

Silvia shook her head.

The baby squirmed in her arms and smiled. Maddie

searched for any signs of sickness, but her heartbeat was regular. No loss of skin elasticity, or signs of lethargy.

No sign of cholera.

Maddie placed the stethoscope around her neck. "Your baby…she's beautiful. And healthy."

"I know…" Silvia glanced over to where the guards were finishing up their dinner. "I needed an excuse to speak to you away from the fire."

"You said you'd help us escape?"

She nodded and pressed something into Maddie's hands before taking the baby.

Maddie closed her fingers around a set of keys. "Why are you doing this for us? If they catch you…"

Silvia cuddled the child against her chest. "Do you have children?"

Maddie shook her head. "One day, perhaps."

"I told you I've lost three babies. It is something I have to accept. But I waited many years for Jose, and now I have Anita. Her name means cheerful, because she brings me joy. My children are all I have." She looked back up at Maddie in the light of one of the lanterns and caught her gaze. "You helped save my son's life. I want to repay you."

"You could leave with us…" Maddie started, not sure if she was crossing a line she shouldn't.

"Oumar would come after me and take my children. This is my life, and I accept that, but you…you don't deserve to be here."

"But—"

"Please. Go before it is too late for you." Silvia stood up and quickly slid Anita on her back, nuzzled closely against her. She covered the baby's bottom and back with her wide cloth, as she'd done a hundred times before, and then secured it tightly in front so it fit like a sling. "I know my husband. He needs you now, but as soon as this sickness is over, he has told the men he is going to kill you. The vehicle is the white Jeep parked on the south side of the camp, just outside the wall. Take it and get as far away from here as you can."

Maddie was still hesitant. "And if he finds out you have helped us?"

"You don't need to worry. I have made sure he won't be able to trace it back to me. Wait until a couple hours before dawn. Most of the guards will be asleep or drunk by then, and I don't expect Oumar to return until it is light again."

"Thank you."

Maddie watched Silvia walk away, her heart aching for the woman. The tragic loss of three children, an unstable life in the middle of this camp, and now her son's life hanging in the balance.

She slipped her hand inside her pocket and clutched the keys Silvia had given her, praying the woman hadn't just signed her own death warrant. Because if Oumar did find out…

Keep her safe, Lord, please.

She glanced at the simple structure behind her. As a doctor, part of her wanted to help these people no matter who they were. She drew in a deep breath of smoke-tinged air. Patients needed to be checked on, beds needed to be changed and washed and fresh rehydration solution made and distributed.

But the other part of her simply wanted to run.

Which meant any risk they had to take in leaving this place was a risk she was willing to take. But until then, she'd continue treating her patients.

She signaled to one of the guards that she needed Grant's and Antonio's help and then gave them instructions on how to mix up another batch of the rehydration formula.

"Is her baby okay?" Grant asked, washing his hands in the boiled water Maddie set in front of him and Antonio.

"So far there are no signs of the cholera."

"That's good."

"It is." She handed him a clean plastic container for the mixture and then pressed the keys into the palm of his hand. "But that's not all she wanted."

The question in Grant's eyes vanished as he realized what she'd given him. "Where did she get these?"

"I didn't ask."

"But you trust her?"

"We have to. I helped save her son. Now she believes she owes me a debt."

"If they catch us escaping, they will kill us," he said.

Maddie paused. "According to Silvia, they will kill us anyway."

Around half past four the next morning, Grant clutched the keys to the Jeep in his hand as they made their way out of the camp. He'd insisted they each take turns sleeping a couple hours before they left. But instead of getting any rest, he'd watched Maddie toss and turn on the thin mat, knowing that if she wasn't awake thinking of their escape, she was dreaming about it.

Now, with the sunrise still a couple of hours away, thunderclouds continued to roll in above them, blotting out the moon and stars and casting their early morning escape in darkness. He was praying the blackness of the night would work to their advantage.

Pressing his hand lightly against the small of Maddie's back, he guided her along the edges of the compound toward the south wall, with Antonio and Ana following right behind them. Except for the hum of an insect and the occasional howl of some nocturnal creature in the distance, silence surrounded them. A guard dozed beside the orange embers of the fire that had yet to go out, unaware his prisoners had just slipped past him.

Twenty yards ahead, something rustled to their left. Grant stopped and held up his hand for them to wait as he searched the darkness for another guard in front of them. He'd studied their patterns and come to the conclusion that they must be more lax when Oumar was gone. Though, in reality, there was little need for tight security. Even beyond these walls there was nothing but more jungles that eventually led to the white sands of the island's shoreline. And no real presence of the law until one reached the mainland.

Not seeing anyone, he nodded for them to continue. He couldn't help but wonder—not for the first time— if Oumar's wife was leading them into a trap. But he knew he had to trust Maddie's instincts. And the motivations of a mother who'd almost lost her child tonight.

"You okay?" he asked her as they paused at the unguarded wall.

"I will be, once we make it out of here."

He caught the fear in her voice, and knew her heart must be pounding and her adrenaline pumping. He wished he could simply whisk her away to safety in Colton's airplane, as he'd planned, but now even once they distanced themselves from the compound this wouldn't be over. He had to find a way to get her off this island.

He pressed his hand against her back for reassurance. "We're almost there."

On the other side of the wall, they hurried toward the place Silvia had told them to go. There were no signs of any of the guards. No signs that anyone had even noticed their middle-of-the-night escape.

The Jeep was where she told them it would be. Now all they had to do was get out of here and make it across the island to the ferry.

Grant slipped into the driver's seat and attempted to start the engine while Maddie got Ana settled into the backseat.

The engine sputtered and choked, trying to start. Nothing. His heart raced. Someone was going to hear his attempts.

"What's wrong?" Antonio asked, climbing into the front passenger seat.

Grant turned the key again. "I don't know. It's not starting."

"Try it again," Antonio said.

"I am."

He glanced into the rearview mirror and started praying. Ironic how catastrophes quickly brought people to their knees. He couldn't even remember the last time he'd prayed this much.

"Do you see anyone out there?" Grant asked.

Antonio studied the darkness around them. "No. Not yet."

Grant tried a fourth time. The engine sputtered and then roared to life. Letting out a whoosh of air, he shifted the car into first and turned on the vehicle's parking lights. Half a tank of gas should easily get them all the way to the ferry crossing.

"Antonio?" he said, stepping on the gas and heading down the rutted path that led away from the compound. "I might be the driver, but you're going to have to help me find our way out of here."

"There's a dirt road up ahead to your right. According to the map I have, it will take us across the island lengthwise, and we'll end up at the port, where we can try to catch the ferry."

There were no guarantees. He knew that. But that didn't stop him from feeling the weight of responsibility for everyone in the car pulling on him. Because the variables of this escape were too numerous to count. They'd be driving through a drug-trafficking hub that had no law and for the moment no way for them to communicate with the outside world.

"What about land mines?" Maddie asked, adding another worry to his growing list. "After last night…"

"If we stay on the dirt roads we should be okay," Antonio said.

Grant wanted to laugh. Calling *this* a road was a joke. He double-checked to ensure the car was in four-wheel drive. The vehicle bounced under them as he fought the loose sand in order to stay on the narrow path without running into a bush or a tree. Which meant he couldn't go faster than ten miles an hour. And even at that slow speed, with no shock absorbers to cushion the deep ruts, they could feel every bump beneath them.

"How long?" Maddie asked.

Grant glanced at the backseat where she sat with Ana's head resting in her lap, while holding on to the armrest with her free hand, knowing she was worried about her patient.

"If you need to stop..." Grant began, understanding the effects of cholera, but knowing they weren't far away enough from the compound to even consider stopping yet.

"She said she's okay. For now."

"In the dark and with these roads in such bad condition, it's going to take us a couple of hours," Antonio said. "While most of this island is uninhabited by the general population, there's a small town where we can stop and try to call for help. It isn't too far from where we should be able to find a boat out of here."

Headlights flashed in the rearview mirror.

"Grant..." Maddie sucked in a breath of air. "There's someone behind us."

"Hang on." Grant pushed on the gas, still fighting to keep the tires in the ruts.

"The main road has to be just ahead of us," Antonio said. "It not paved, but you'll be able to drive a little faster."

"Maybe it's not them," Maddie said. "Maybe it's just another driver."

"Not out here," Antonio said. "The only vehicles you'll see belong to them."

Grant glanced in his rearview mirror. "Maddie, I want you and Ana to stay down."

He didn't have to verbalize what he was thinking. The other car presumably had weapons. All they had was a stolen Jeep.

He leaned forward as the headlights caught the turn-off onto the main road up ahead. The Jeep fishtailed as he made the turn, then jerked to a stop as the engine died. Grant quickly restarted the engine and tried to move forward, but the wheels started spinning. He banged on the steering wheel and then quickly threw the car into Reverse and backed up. The quickest way to get completely stuck was to let the tires spin. They didn't have time to dig the Jeep out of a hole.

He eased off the gas. "Come on…come on…"

"Grant…" Maddie's voice was laced in panic.

"How close are they?" Grant asked.

"I don't know, but they're gaining on us," she said.

Antonio jumped out of the car.

"Antonio!" Grant shouted, still trying to get the vehicle unstuck.

"Give me ten seconds."

"We don't have ten seconds," Grant shouted, but Antonio was already gone.

Grant shifted into first again and then eased on the pedal. This time the car moved forward enough to get them free.

Antonio jumped back into the car, slamming his door shut. "Get us out of here."

Grant eased down slowly on the gas, then sped onto the main road. The headlights were still behind them.

"What did you just do?" he asked, picking up speed on the packed dirt road.

Antonio gripped the dashboard. "There were a couple fallen palm tree fronds on the side of the road. They happen to have these sharp thorns on the back of them that can be extremely painful if you step on them. They've also been known to puncture a tire or two. I thought if I laid them across the road it might delay our friends. With a little luck, they won't even see them."

"I knew there was a good reason for bringing you along." Grant chuckled.

"It looks like they've stopped," Maddie said a few seconds later.

"Which means you, my friend, just bought us some more time." Grant looked back in his rearview mirror as the other vehicle's headlights began to fade into the distance.

But while they might have lost them, this was far from over. They were unarmed in a territory that was not only unfamiliar, but run by local drug traffickers. How many more second chances to get out alive were they going to get?

FIVE

A pinkish glow along the horizon signaled another African dawn, allowing Grant to finally catch his first glimpse of the Atlantic beyond the thick jungle interior and surrounding green coastal plains. Beyond the waves lapping up the shoreline, fishermen bobbed along the water in dugout canoes.

He glanced in his rearview mirror, looking for signs that they were being followed, something not too difficult to do on the current flat terrain. In the past hour he hadn't seen any other vehicles. Maybe the other driver had simply given up his pursuit, but he knew this wasn't over. He had to get Maddie off this island.

According to Antonio's calculations, the closest fishing village was now only a few kilometers away. While still off the typical tourist map, for those looking to venture off the beaten track the dozens of islands sprinkled along the Atlantic coast were a perfect choice. For someone trying to run, though, options suddenly became severely limited. A flight off the island, if even possible, was still their quickest and best chance. Otherwise they were going to have to secure a boat.

He glanced over at Maddie, who had switched seats

with Antonio thirty minutes ago and now dozed beside him in the front seat. Her plan had been to keep him awake, but both the physical and emotional toll of the past few days had clearly stretched her to her limits. He forced himself to keep his eye on the road and not on her. Because he'd forgotten how beautiful she was. Even after all she'd been through, there was still a healthy glow to her cheeks, coupled with her long dark hair and tan skin, thanks to her Brazilian mother.

But he shouldn't be thinking about how pretty she was. He was only here to repay a debt to a friend. Nothing more. And besides, once he got her home, her life would continue on without him. She'd go back to her own world, and he'd go back to his. Experience had taught him that. Women tended not to fall for men who constantly put their lives at risk. And while some might call him a hero, when it came to marriage he couldn't forget that they also wanted someone who would settle down and give them a sense of stability.

He'd spent the past ten plus years living everywhere from Sierra Leone to Bosnia and educating soldiers on how to detect and deactivate mines. Not to mention he himself was out in the field helping to remove the live explosives. The word *stable* didn't exactly describe his life.

Maddie shifted in her seat beside him as he swerved to avoid a pothole on the narrow dirt road.

"Sorry." She tugged on her seat-belt strap and sat forward. "I must have fallen asleep again."

"Don't worry about it. You're exhausted."

"Yes, but I'm supposed to help you stay awake. You should have woken me up."

"I don't know…you looked so peaceful."

"Was I snoring?"

"Just once or twice."

"Sorry." She yawned and shot him a sleepy smile. "I feel like I'm back in med school with this sleep-deprived fog over me. What time is it?"

"Close to seven. The sun will be coming up soon, though yesterday's storms seem to be picking up strength today. There are a lot of dark clouds rumbling out there."

She leaned back into her seat and groaned. "Normally I love a good thunderstorm, but here the rains just add to the humidity."

"The weather here takes a bit of getting used to, doesn't it?"

Maddie laughed. "That's an understatement. Especially for someone used to cold winters and lots of snow. Between the rains and the high humidity, I don't know... I can't say it's something I'll ever get accustomed to. I remember when I first arrived here with our team. We'd left Chicago in the middle of a blizzard but then landed in the middle of a heat wave. No electricity meant no fans or air conditioners. I would gladly have given a month's salary for a bag of ice and a liter of Coke."

"I admit since arriving here, I've dreamed of a couple feet of snow outside my back door more than once."

She let out a low chuckle, but he didn't need to look at her to know she had more on her mind than just the changes in weather.

"So what happens now?" She stared out across the shoreline beside him and tapped her fingers against the armrest. The colors of the sunrise spilled out across the water. "We might have managed to lose them, but somehow I don't think they're the kind of men who just give up."

"I don't, either. As soon as we get to town, we'll need to find a way to contact the embassy in Dakar and your aid organization. And I need to see if I can get ahold of my pilot friend again. Hopefully we can come up with another rendezvous point. If not, we'll see if we can hire a speedboat, which will be a lot faster than a fishing boat, assuming we can come up with a driver and enough cash."

He hated making plans on the fly, but that's all he was working with at the moment.

He glanced at the side-view mirror. There were still no signs of anyone following them, but he knew there was only one way across this island. If they decided to come after them, tracking down where they were wouldn't be hard.

"What about contacting the local authorities on the island?" she asked.

"You might not have noticed, but it's a bit like the Wild West out here."

"What, there isn't any 911 service out here?" She laughed, but he didn't miss the sarcasm in her voice.

Even if they wanted to contact the local authorities from the mainland, the drug-trafficking hub had no police and no communication equipment. And it wasn't a whole lot better on the mainland. They only had a handful of detention centers, and no long-term plans to keep criminals locked up.

"Things are slowly changing," he said, hoping to reassure her. "Both Portugal and Brazil are helping with the training of police units as well as improving surveillance equipment and phone links between the islands and the mainland. But in the meantime—"

"We're pretty much on our own," she said, finishing his sentence for him.

"That's a pretty fair assessment. And at the moment, not much of a rescue plan, I'm afraid. Especially when plan A—that included a plane ride out of here—might prove to be impossible."

"And plan B?" she asked, turning back to him. "Do you think it's going to be any more reliable?"

Grant tapped the steering wheel. "You mean driving this secondhand—stolen, I might add—vehicle?"

"When you put it that way, the reliability factor kind of loses its punch." Maddie laughed, but her smile quickly faded. "What happens if we can't find one of those speedboats?"

"Then we go to option C. Haven't you ever taken the ferry to one of these islands?"

"I was planning to before all this happened, though somehow this wasn't exactly the way I pictured it. I've heard, though—minus the whole abduction part, of course—that it's an experience that shouldn't be missed."

"Yeah… I'm thinking most tourists would prefer to avoid that whole abduction scenario." He chuckled, liking the fact that despite everything she'd been through, she'd still managed to hold on to her sense of humor. "I took the ferry once, on a long weekend off between projects. It was slow, but relatively safe and cheap."

The four-hundred-dollar one-way ticket for a speedboat had been way out of he and his friends' price range, and the third option, one of the long wooden boats the locals used, had a disturbing tendency to sink when overloaded with people and goods. He'd decided that idea was out of the question as well, and settled on what turned out to be a seven-hour ride that only set him back a few dollars.

"What were your first impressions?"

"Besides the long ferry ride that turned out to be an adventure in itself, the people were friendly, the food fantastic and I stumbled across some of the most beautiful beaches I'd ever seen. I even hired a bike and rode to see a pod of rare saltwater hippos."

A smile played on her lips again, as she turned around to check on Ana. "Maybe when this is all over I'll discover this place my way, though I'm thinking the next time I'm in the mood for a bit of sun and beach, I just might head for the Caribbean."

"I wouldn't blame you at all."

Ana shifted in the backseat.

"Is she still asleep?" Grant asked.

"Both of them are."

Grant snagged another glance at Maddie's profile and caught the determined tilt of her chin. Her hands sat clenched in her lap, as she continued to check the side mirror for signs they were being followed. She was strong yet vulnerable at the same time. So much the same woman he remembered. And all the things that had impressed him back then continued to impress him today. Her determination and confidence. Her professionalism and yet at the same time her ability to be completely down-to-earth.

But as much as he was enjoying talking with her— and as much as he wished they were here enjoying those pristine beaches and not in the car fighting for their lives—the reality of their situation couldn't be dismissed.

"There's something I need to talk to you about," he started cautiously, his hands gripping the steering wheel as he kept driving past acres of mangroves and palm trees. Beyond the beach to his right he caught glimpses of other islands in the distance. Maybe his fears were based on nothing, but they couldn't afford to make any assumptions. Not yet anyway. "I've been thinking about Sam. I'd like to know more about him and what he said to you."

"I'm not sure what else to tell you." A touch of concern laced her voice. "He was admitted into the hospital around seven when I treated him for a gunshot wound. I checked on him a couple times after his surgery while doing my rounds that night. The first time he was still unconscious. Weak, but stable. The second time is when he spoke to me. Two hours later he passed away. We did everything we could, but the internal damage was too severe."

"What exactly did he say to you?"

"At first I thought he was just rambling, because nothing he said made sense. He just sputtered words about drug flights, rebels, trafficking. Then he seemed to have a moment of clarity."

"And that's when he mentioned the evidence he had?"

"Yeah. He told me about someone high up in the State Department who's profiting from the drug trafficking in this country. And he had evidence to prove what he had discovered."

"The flash drive."

"Yes."

"Anything else?"

"He mentioned some girl, but I can't remember her name. Kristen… Christine…something like that. He wanted me to find her."

"To tell her what happened at the end of his life?" Grant asked.

"That's what I assumed, but I don't understand. Why all the questions?"

"It's just this…nagging feeling I can't shake."

The smell of salt water tinged the air through the open window. Now that they were closer to the nearest town, they were beginning to pass mud-walled, thatched-roof huts surrounded by palm and mango trees. Even at this early hour, people were already up. A woman was hanging laundry on an old electric line. A couple boys played soccer in the dirt. Women walked along the side of the road carrying buckets of water on their heads, while men rode rickety bicycles toward town.

"Okay, explain what you mean," she said.

He nodded, appreciating the fact she wasn't ready to dismiss his concerns. "I've assumed from the beginning— and perhaps you have as well—that you were kidnapped because they needed a doctor in the camp. Which makes sense. But the more I think about it, the more I'm not willing to simply ignore the possibility that you having that flash drive doesn't somehow figure into all of this."

Maddie tugged on the seat-belt strap and weighed her response. It wasn't the first time she'd questioned why they'd taken her, but up until this point it hadn't seemed to matter. All she'd really known was that her skills as a doctor had been keeping her alive.

"So you're saying I was—am—a target because of Sam and the information I have."

"I'm saying it's a possibility."

"I agree that when you look at everything involved, it does seem like too much of a coincidence that Sam and this flash drive aren't somehow a part of my abduction, but I'm still not sure how it's possible. I don't know how anyone could have overhead our conversation."

"You're positive that another patient, or nurse or a visitor couldn't have seen the two of you talking? Someone who knew Sam had this information, and realized it was something he might pass on knowing he was dying?

She stared out the window as they passed a large green peanut field. Muddy brown paths lead away from it, disappearing into forest beyond. "No… Yes… I don't know… I guess it's possible. But I'm not sure why it matters."

"Maybe it doesn't. I don't know. But it would be nice to know who or what we're up against. If we're dealing with local drug traffickers, they might not come after you, because they prefer to keep a low profile. But if we're dealing with someone powerful who's trying to cover his back…"

The conclusion she hadn't wanted to acknowledge swept through her. If some high-up government official thought she could put him behind bars, he would come after her.

But still…

"I can't deny the validity to what you're saying, but I still don't think anyone knows what Sam told me."

"Then lets go through the facts of what happened the day they took you."

Maddie paused as they passed an old abandoned hotel. She didn't want to remember that moment again. Like the mainland, apparently even the isolated islands held glimpses of the Portuguese influence on the country. Many of the once-impressive colonial buildings, abandoned after independence, were now nothing more than crumbling relics from the past. Like the road of mud and shells they were driving on now.

She fought to keep her mind focused. She wanted to believe that he'd rescued her and now everything was going to be okay again. And because every night since that afternoon when they'd taken her, she'd woken up in a sweat from nightmares. The terror of being shoved into a car. Watching Gavin slump to the ground. And feeling the blindfold slip over her eyes.

No. She didn't want to go there again.

During her orientation, she'd been warned that she needed to be aware of her own personal security, but that violence against foreigners wasn't usual. Most of the rules they'd laid out were simply common sense. While serious crime tended to be fairly low, they were to be aware of pickpockets who were rampant. They'd also been advised to avoid any demonstrations and have an exit strategy in case of an emergency.

And that's exactly what she'd discovered. The people she worked with, as well as the patients she treated on a daily basis, had welcomed her warmly. She'd never felt threatened. Never felt in danger. Which was why, in the ten months she'd lived in the country, she'd never felt afraid as she had during the time they'd grabbed her, or in the days that had followed.

"Maddie?"

She shook her head. Running, even if it was only in her mind, wasn't going to change their situation.

"I'm sorry—"

"It's okay. I know this is hard on you. But we need to know what we're up against."

She nodded and forced herself to step back into the memories. "Gavin and I were on our way from the hospital back to the row of rooms we rented a few blocks away. It had been raining all day. I remember a car drove by too fast and splashed mud across my scrub pants. I was frustrated because I was tired and now I was going to have to go and wash them out. Seems petty, looking back. A couple minutes later, another car stopped and a man got out. I didn't think anything about it until he pulled out a gun and asked me if I was Dr. Gilbert."

Maddie closed her eyes wishing she could block it all out, but it was still there, as fresh as it had been the second it happened. The smell of rain. Mud oozing over the tops of her shoes. And the sound of a gunshot.

"They shot him. Gavin fell backward onto the side of the street. I pulled away from whoever was gripping my arm to try to save him, but Gavin was already dead." Maddie stared out the window as they drove past a woman carrying bananas on her head. Cool air from the sea blew across her face. The scent of salt water heavy in the air. "I remember feeling like my mind couldn't keep up with what was happening. Couldn't accept it. They could have let him go and just taken me, but for some reason they didn't."

"Did he try to fight back?"

"I don't rememb… Yes." Somehow she'd forgotten that part until now. "He tried to pull me out of the car."

Her fingers automatically reached up to touch her

forearm where there was still a tint of bruise from where they'd grabbed her. He'd tried to save her.

"His death was my fault." She ran her fingers down her arm. They were getting closer to town now. Mud huts were sprinkled throughout the lush terrain. "I thought they killed him because he wasn't a doctor, but they killed him simply because he was with me."

Grant swerved to the left to avoid a deep rut in the road. "Don't even go there, Maddie. None of this was your fault. What happened next?"

"They put a blindfold on me and drove off. Fifteen… twenty minutes later, we stopped at what had to be a landing strip and got into an airplane. Because of the short distance, I guessed they'd taken me to one of these islands. Ana confirmed it later."

"And the flash drive. Did anyone ever ask you about Sam or the information he had?"

"No. All I was told was that people were dying and if I wanted to live, I needed to find a way to save them." Maddie glanced down at the locket still hanging around her neck. "I'd planned to meet my supervisor that evening and tell him about Sam and the flash drive. I never had a chance."

Had someone stopped her on purpose? Or had it been nothing more than a coincidence?

"Don't you think if they were aware I'd spoken to Sam they would have tried to find out what I knew?"

"I'm not sure," he said.

"Well, I'm not, either. But what I do know is that this country is full of good people, like Silvia. It's people like Oumar who spoil it," she said. "Coming here I was completely out of my comfort zone, and yet I've sat and eaten in their homes, listened to their stories, cried with them over their losses. It's a place where people have so little and yet it has so much to offer at the same time. In the ten months that I've been here, I know I've learned more from them than I'll ever be able to give back."

"I agree and maybe that's why I keep coming back. Africa tends to grab on to a piece of your heart and doesn't let go. We should be almost to the town that has a market where we can buy some breakfast," he said, changing the subject for the moment. "We'll stop there, then drive on to the island's port."

"So have you come to any conclusions?" she asked.

"I think we have to assume that someone at least believes you talked with Sam. And that we can't ignore the possibility that there are some heavy hitters involved who orchestrated your kidnapping."

"Like whoever's name is on the flash drive."

Grant nodded. "Exactly."

"But why bring me to a rebel camp to treat their sick?"

"I don't know. Maybe that wasn't supposed to be what happened. Those involved with the drug running tend to keep low profiles. All I can figure is they realized you were a doctor and decided you could serve two purposes."

"If this is true, then I'm still a loose end." Maddie clasped the locket between her fingers.

He reached out and squeezed her other hand. "Which is why we're going to get you off this island and find out what's on that flash drive."

SIX

Grant drove through the small town that was nestled along the shoreline, praying this was going to be their ticket out of here. From the air, the dozens of islands surrounding them looked like a pile of gems against the brilliant blue waters of the Atlantic Ocean. A stunning contrast to the bleak Sahara Desert farther north.

Most of those living on these islands had little need—or desire—of the outside world. They grew their own rice while acres of palm groves produced oil and palm wine. Mudflats contained shellfish and the sea provided a ready supply of fish. The outside world had tried to change that self-sufficiency, beginning with a fifteenth-century Portuguese explorer who was promptly killed for his efforts to conquer them. Today, there were only subtle signs of European influence, primarily from the worn-out buildings abandoned after independence.

Grant parked along the edge of a narrow street that was filled mainly with pedestrians and sellers and turned off the motor, realizing how nothing had changed since the last time he'd been here.

Antonio rested his hand on the door handle in the backseat. "I'll go talk to my friend and see if I can find someone to arrange a private boat off this island. Meet you back here in ten…fifteen minutes top."

Maddie glanced at Ana, as Antonio headed out of the vehicle, shutting the door behind him. "Do you feel up to walking around and finding something to eat?"

The young girl nodded, though from her glassy eyes it was clear she still wasn't feeling well. "I am hungry."

"Sounds like a good sign to me, doctor."

"It is," Maddie said, but he caught the hesitation in her voice. "But do you think we should get out of the car? I'd really like to stretch my legs, but if it's not safe…"

The busy road where he'd parked was flanked by run-down buildings with tin roofs. Along the sides, women sold fish, oysters, shrimp, cashews and palm oil nuts out of colorful plastic tubs. People bustled by past them, buying and selling, completely unaware he and those with him were running for their lives.

He wanted to tell her there was nothing to worry about. That both she and Ana were safe now. But while no one had followed them on the road, there were still no guarantees that the men after them weren't still out there. He glanced toward the mainland. The thirty miles of open sea to the capital had never seemed so far. I think we'll be okay," he said finally. "If they're determined to find you, it won't matter if you're walking down the street or sitting in one of their vehicles. We just need to keep our eyes open, and pay attention to what's going on around us."

Maddie stayed close beside him, her arm around Ana's shoulder. He wished they could simply blend into the crowd, but for the two of them that wasn't possible.

He studied the busy street, looking for anything that seemed off. He wished they had time to eat a proper meal. There wasn't time to hunt down a restaurant, but at least the rebels hadn't discovered the hidden zipper in his cargo pants where he'd stashed some of his money. A glance into a small store offered canned sardines, tomato paste, spaghetti noodles and powered milk on its shelves, but they had no way to cook anything. Instead, they hurried into the open market where they could find a better selection of "fast food." A handful of change bought them some bread, a half dozen boiled eggs, and a bagful of roasted cashews.

"How much for your cell phone?" he asked the woman tending the store, "I'll give you two times what it's worth."

She looked up at him like he was crazy, hesitated for a couple seconds and then handed him the phone. Though having it didn't guarantee the ability to get through.

He looked at Maddie and caught the look of concern on her face.

"What's wrong?" he asked.

"I've been keeping my eye on two men just down the street. I've seen them move from store to store like they're looking for someone."

He glanced back at where she was looking, but they must have already gone into one of the stores.

"Did they look familiar?" he asked.

Maddie nodded.

"I've seen them too," Ana said. "They were at the camp."

Grant felt his jaw tense, as he steered them in the opposite direction, back through the market. "They've got to be the men who were following us. Which means we need to get back to the Jeep. Now."

Grant tried not to worry as he hurried them through

a maze of sellers, the rank smell of salted fish lying in the sun to dry filling his nose. Past piles of fat pumpkins, cucumbers and mounds of cashews. He dialed his pilot friend again, praying that the strings he'd had to pull were going to end up paying off.

"So much for a phone," he said, frustration burrowing through him.

"You still can't get ahold of him?" Maddie asked as they left the crowded market behind. He could see their car now, standing out in a sea of pedestrians at the end of the street. But no sign of the men.

"The call won't even go through." Grant let out an exasperated sigh. "I'm trying to send a text message as well. Hopefully it will go out eventually."

When he'd decided to plan a rescue, he'd known they'd have to be flexible and that getting her off this island wasn't going to be simple. But he'd gone ahead, praying their quickly laid plans would work. Colton Landry, his pilot friend, hadn't hesitated when Grant had asked him for help, even knowing that any part he played in this rescue attempt was a risk. But now he couldn't help but wonder if his friend had tried to land that plane... And if the same men who were after them had been there waiting.

Antonio was crossing the road and making his way toward them.

"Did you find a boat?" Grant asked as they continued together toward the car and he pulled the keys from his pocket.

"Yes and no. There's a storm coming in, and the sea's too rough right now for smaller boat. We'd have to wait until this afternoon...maybe even tomorrow."

Grant frowned. "We don't have time to wait until

tomorrow. We spotted two of the men from the camp on the other side of the market."

And in a place this small, there would be no place to hide.

"So what are our other options?" Grant asked.

"The ferry is arriving this morning with fuel and supplies. As soon as it off-loads, it's going to return to the mainland, which means we're going to have to hurry in order to catch it."

"And we're what…thirty minutes away still?"

Antonio nodded.

Grant let out a huff. A speedboat could have gotten them to the mainland in just over an hour, while the ferry could take up to eight hours.

"You're sure the ferry's the best option?" Maddie asked, trying to maneuver around a woman carrying a stack of firewood on her head. "If there's a bad storm coming in, I don't want to be out there on that water."

"It might not be the best," Antonio said, "but it's our only one at this point. It's equipped with GPS and can handle the rough seas. Considering the circumstances, rough seas are the least of our problems,"

"No kidding," Grant said.

"There's more. I just spoke to my friend who lives here," Antonio continued. "He's the one who helped me find where you were being held, Maddie. He heard this morning that the local authorities have been told to bring you in for questioning, and I don't mean in order to stage their own rescue."

"Then why?" Maddie's voice rose a notch.

"For stealing a vehicle and kidnapping Ana."

"Kidnapping… You've got to be kidding me," Grant

said. "We rescued Ana from a rebel camp, and they accuse us of kidnapping?"

"She asked to come with us," Maddie said.

"Corruption runs deep," Antonio said. "The drug traffickers have deep pockets and if someone wants to keep you quiet, Maddie…"

"That means we can't go to the police here on the island," Grant said.

"The only upside is that communication is pretty much limited to two-way radios, and their manpower is just as limited. But my advice is that we get to that ferry as fast as we can to ensure we get on. The next one won't get here until Sunday, which means we'd be stuck on the island until the weather calms down."

Grant started back toward the car through the crowded street and stopped. Ana, who had been beside Maddie only seconds ago, wasn't there. "Maddie… where's Ana?"

Maddie turned to where Ana had been standing beside her. "Ana?"

Grant was right. She was gone.

Maddie sucked in a deep breath, trying not to panic as she searched the crowded street. "Ana… Ana? She was just here…"

"Which means she couldn't have gone far," Antonio said. "We'll find her." Maddie ran back toward the side street where they'd been standing, knowing Ana was both sick and scared, but there was no sign of her. She turned in a slow circle, trying to catch sight of the bright orange dress Ana had been wearing. Antonio had to be right, though. She couldn't have gone far. She could easily have seen something and wandered off to check it out. Or maybe even simply gone to sit down. Because the alternative—the possibility that they'd taken her—was too terrifying.

"I never should have taken her out of that car," Maddie said, turning back to Grant and Antonio.

"Let's split up again and meet back here in five minutes," Antonio said. "The two of you go check the market. I'll check the other direction."

Grant gripped her elbow and started walking back toward the market where they'd bought the boiled eggs and bread she was still carrying in the plastic bag. "We're going to find her," he said, trying to reassure her.

She bit her tongue, wanting to believe his promise, but knowing that he'd been right about coincidences. This couldn't be just another one of them. "Do you think they took her?"

"No." Grant grabbed her hand and hurried through a narrow side street that ran along the edge of the marketplace. "Because she's not who they really want. If they'd found her…they would have found us as well."

"But they're still out there, and she's out there."

"I know."

Maddie wasn't even going to verbalize what would happen if they didn't find her. They needed to get off the island, but she had no intention of leaving Ana behind.

They were back in the market again. The scent of the coming rains, brought by the breeze from the ocean, was competing with the rows of fish for sale.

"Her fever was rising last time I felt her skin," Maddie said. "If we don't find her…"

"We're going to find her."

Maddie stopped in front of the woman who'd sold them the eggs. "I'm looking for the girl that was with

me. Her name's Ana. Have you seen her? We were sep-
arated in the crowd."

"I'm sorry. No."

They continued down the rows, asking people if
they'd seen her, all the way to the end of the market,
but there was no sign of her. Only the gray sea spreading out before them in the distance.

"If she came back this way," Grant said, "someone
would have seen her."

"Then where do we go?"

Maddie stared at the ocean. The storm brewed in
the distance. Lightning flashed. One of a dozen baobab
trees found on the island stood near the shoreline, its
bare and twisted rootlike branches spreading out beyond
the thick trunk. Eerie and foreboding. As much as she
didn't want to be stuck on this island, neither was she
sure she wanted to be out on the water during a storm.

"Wait a minute…" Grant said.

"What it is?"

"I think she's out there. On the sand, to the left."

Maddie turned and caught the color of orange fluttering in the wind. Grant squeezed her hand and starting running toward the beach. There were cows lying
in the sand. A forgotten pirogue carved from the trunk
of a Kapok tree. Thousands of fiddler crabs hurried to
burrow into the sand at their approach, while a heron
stood unmoving, ready to catch his breakfast.

Ana sat facing the sea while the wind whipped at
her dress and braids.

Maddie fell down on her knees on the sand in front
of her. "Ana…are you okay?"

Silent tears streamed down Ana's face. "I'm sorry.
I thought I lost you. I turned around and…you were

gone. There were so many people. I was so afraid they were going to take me back. I saw those men standing beside the car…"

"No one's taking you back." Maddie sat down beside her and cradled her against her chest.

"My grandmother's out there somewhere. I thought if I waited long enough a boat would come and take me to her."

"Come on." Maddie helped her stand up. "You're safe now, Ana. And we're going to help you find your grandmother."

SEVEN

Grant snacked on a handful of cashews while driving along the muddy dirt road toward the port where they planned to catch the ferry. He hated the uncertainty of what was ahead. The dark clouds were coming closer, hovering over the sea that had turned a dreary shade of gray beneath what was left of the morning sunlight. His mind churned over the details of their dilemma. With local officials looking for them, this situation had become far bigger than just a camp of insurgents needing a doctor. Which meant it was only a matter of time until they were found. He needed to get them off this island—even though getting to the mainland still didn't guarantee Maddie's safety. They were going to have to find a place to go where they could figure out what to do with the information she'd been handed.

Grant switched on his wipers as drops of rain began to splash onto the windshield. Two men, possibly more, had died over the information she'd been given. Which meant they were going to have to bring what Sam had discovered to light. And bring whoever was behind all of this to justice.

The narrow dirt road snaked in front of them, while

green rice fields surrounded them on one side, the ocean on the other. Antonio's friends had managed to buy them some time, sending the men after them to the other side of the island. Now all they needed to do right now was make sure they got on that ferry.

Grant slowed down, to avoid a large rut in the road ahead, and then came to a stop. It wasn't just another rut. A huge section of the road was gone.

"Grant…what's wrong?" Maddie leaned forward between the two front seats.

"The road's washed away."

"Washed away?"

Grant jumped out of the vehicle and walked toward the gully. The washed-out section spanned the length of the road as far as he could see in both directions. Going across the fifteen-foot gap in the road wasn't an option. Which meant the only way was around.

Antonio stepped out of the car behind Grant. "Talk about bad timing. I knew there'd been a lot of rain these past few days, but no one in town mentioned a washout."

"Do you think we can go around?" Grant asked.

"I don't know. Driving toward the sea isn't an option. I think we're going to have to find a way through one of the rice field paths."

"Grant?"

He turned back to where Maddie stood, the wind tugging at her long hair. She was depending on him to get her and Ana out of here alive.

"Let's get back in the car." He tried to mask the concern in his voice as he headed back toward her and the car. Then he stopped beside her. "We're going to get you out of here, Maddie. Home by Christmas, remember?"

She nodded.

He squeezed her hand, wanting to assure her, but knowing he was making promises he wasn't sure he could keep. They needed to make it to that ferry, get off this island and make it to the capital, all without running into the wrong people.

And time was running out.

Back in the car, Grant found a narrow path that ran parallel to where the road had washed out that he hoped would eventually get them back to the main road. Bushes and shrubs scraped against the sides of the vehicle. He glanced back at Maddie, her fingers gripping the armrest. Her expression sober. Once he'd found out where they were holding her, his plan had seemed straightforward, though admittedly risky. A swift night rescue with a plane waiting in the wings. He'd counted on the element of surprise to tip things in his favor.

But so far, nothing had gone as planned. And not only had his rescue attempt gone wrong, his heart had somehow managed to get tangled up in the process as well. Maddie Gilbert. His best friend's little sister. He'd come to bring her home. Nothing more. But instead those brief smiles she'd given him, in the face of such danger no less, had managed to start chipping away at the wall around his heart—

He felt a sharp tug on the left side of the car. The suspension vibrated as Grant stepped on the brakes. *You've got to be kidding me, God...*

He shifted the car into Neutral and pulled on the emergency break. "I think we've got a flat tire."

"What?" Antonio said.

Maddie and Antonio jumped out of the car behind him. Sure enough...the back tire was flat.

Okay, I could really use some help here, God...

"This is crazy," Maddie said.

"And we're not going anywhere, for the moment. I don't even know if this car has a jack, let alone if the spare tire has any air."

Grant headed around the car to the passenger side and thankfully found the jack under the seat. "How much time do we have, Antonio?"

"Not enough time for something else to go wrong. They're going to leave as soon as they can off-load everything from the ferry. And with the storm coming in, they'll be in a hurry to get back to the mainland."

"Need some help?" Maddie asked. "My stepfather taught me to change a tire before I got my license."

"Yes, thanks," Grant said.

"Better you than me, then," Antonio said. "I might be able to deactivate a land mine, but I'll leave changing a tire to the experts."

Maddie laughed. "If you'll find Ana a dry place to sit and see if she'll take some more of the rehydration drink."

"Tell me about Antonio," Maddie said a minute later while she worked to loosen the spare tire secured to the back hatch of the vehicle. "Where did you meet him?"

"Right here in Guinea-Bissau. He was one of the recruits I worked with when I was assigned here to teach how to clear land mines. He was—and still is—one of the best. He had a degree in Development Studies from the UK, so was well educated and already spoke English perfectly when we first met. We've become close friends over the years."

"He's connected with Ana," Maddie said, glancing where he'd found a place for her to sit and was now encouraging her to drink.

"I'm not surprised. He's always been great with kids. He and his wife have twin daughters of their own. They just turned four. But they've also taken in three older siblings, two nieces and a nephew whose parents died a few years back. He's a good man." Grant crouched down beside the flat. "We're going to need something to stabilize the jack in this sand once I loosen these lug nuts."

She stood next to him, hands on her hips, lips pursed. "Like what?"

"In ideal conditions I'd take a proper 3-ton jack on a flat surface, but we're not exactly looking at ideal conditions, are we?"

Maddie laughed. "Trust me, after living here these past few months and working in less than ideal conditions, I'm used to improvising. How about a floor mat?"

"I'll take about anything at this point. Let's give it a try."

She opened up the passenger door, pulled out the mat and handed it to him. Then she slid the spare wheel under the chassis rails next to where he was going to jack up the car. "On the off chance that the jack decides not to cooperate."

"Smart move," he said, setting up the jack. "Is your stepdad still into cars the way he used to be?"

"Oh, yeah. He's got an old vintage Mustang from the '60s in the garage right now that I've helped him on some. It's a beauty, though I'm not sure he's ever going to finish. I've finally decided he likes the process as much as he likes the cars."

Grant moved to loosen the last lug nut. It was stuck. "I knew that Darren had restored a couple classics, but I didn't remember you being interested in cars."

"Darren had a passion for them, too. For me, I just

enjoyed hanging out with my stepdad on my days off. And since that was what he loved to do, it wasn't hard to pick up a few tips along the way. Though to be honest, I'm perfectly happy to call AAA to take care of any problems back home."

"If only that was an option out here," he said, placing the wrench on the nut and using his full weight to loosen it.

The rain had stopped for the moment, but the wind was kicking up.

"Do you think we're going to make the ferry?" she asked.

"We'll have a better chance if I can get this last lug nut loose…"

"Why don't you try this," she said, handing him a four-way wrench.

He tried to loosen it again with the wrench she'd given him. A second later, the lug nut was free. "You know, you're pretty handy to have around."

Her fingers brushed against his as he handed the wrench back to her. He caught her gaze and felt another chip around his heart fall away.

"There's…um…a streak of dirt across your chin." He reached up to wipe his thumb to brush it off, but only managed to smear it further. He shot her a grin. "Well, it looks like all I've done is make it worse."

"Forget it." Maddie felt her cheeks heat up at his touch and quickly pulled away. But she couldn't escape those blue eyes of his. "As thankful as I am for the clean set of clothes, first on my list when we get off this island is a hot shower."

She quickly positioned herself in front of the side

mirror and did her best to remove the streak of dirt.
And to stop the irregular beating of her heart. She
still wasn't quite sure how he'd managed to affect her
so deeply. All she knew was that he did. And the timing couldn't be worse. She had enough to worry about
without the man beside her making her feel like she
was still that same young girl who'd had a crush on
her older brother's best friend.

"Another few hours and this will all be behind us,"
he said, "and I'll make sure you get your shower."

"I'm counting on it." She managed to rub off the
rest of the dirt. Then she glanced back at him. Part of
her was certain she'd stepped into the Twilight Zone.
Because how else had an ordinary girl managed to get
herself involved with an international drug trafficking
ring? And in the middle of her crisis, how else could
she have found a man who managed to make her heart
feel completely vulnerable? But she had to remember,
Grant had come to rescue her. To make good on a promise to her brother. Nothing more.

"Can I ask you a question?" he asked, sliding the
jack under the frame and turning the lift.

"Of course," she said, pulling her thoughts back to
the present.

"You've told me *how* you came to be here. But *what*
made you chose to come here?"

Maddie hesitated. His question took her off guard.
Maybe it was because she'd spent so much time over
the past few days second-guessing if her decision to
move here really had been the right one. The week before she left, her mother had sat her down and told her
she was throwing her life away. Her fiancé, her job—
everything she had going for her. And Maddie had

understood why. It wasn't as much about Ben or her practice, but instead her mother had been afraid of losing her…like she had Darren.

But as much as she'd understood her mother's fears, she'd known it was a risk she needed to take. She'd lived her life doing what was expected of her, and she'd succeeded. But it had been time to veer off in a direction that was right for her.

She decided to put him off. "I'm not sure it's something I can begin to answer in the span of changing a tire."

He removed the last lug nut and smiled up at her. "Try me."

"Okay." Maybe he was right. Maybe with everything that had happened the past few days, she needed to remember why she'd decided to come in the first place. "I heard this guy speak at a fund-raiser. He'd been working overseas and told a story about three women's experiences with complications during their pregnancies in a place that has one of the highest death rates in the world. And how a new center for pregnant women was saving lives by specializing in high-risk pregnancies. There they received nutritious food and medical supervision that helped detect potential life-threatening complications that were normally diagnosed too late. I sat there, knowing I wanted to be a part of it."

She stopped for a moment as he pulled the flat tire off the rim, and helped switch it out with the spare. "I went home and realized that I'd been living out everyone else's expectations for me. But I was still torn, and I didn't really know what I wanted to do with my skills. I was working for a great practice doing something I loved. I was planning to marry this great guy. It wasn't as if I was unhappy, because I wasn't. But something was missing, and I wanted to find out what else was out there. Sounds crazy, doesn't it?"

Her mother had definitely thought so.

"Actually, not at all," he said, lowering the jack.

"I decided I'd been living my life on the sidelines, taking the easy route. I wasn't living boldly," Maddie continued. "You take risks every day, but I hadn't even stopped to take the time to think about what I really wanted in life. So I started praying that God would open up doors if He wanted me somewhere else. And He did."

"And the location?" Grant asked.

"The place the man spoke about at the fund-raiser was Guinea-Bissau. Since I grew up speaking Portuguese with my mom, it seemed like the right place. Before I knew it I'd called off my engagement with Ben, officially signed up to come here and had bought my plane ticket."

"Any regrets?"

"None, though I'm not sure my family would say the same thing. Especially with all that's happened the past few days. This was my mother's greatest fear. That I'd come here and something would happen to me."

"She's stronger than you think."

"I hope so. Because I saw her go through the loss of my brother. It tore her world in half. And I think made her hold me even tighter."

"What about Ben?" Grant asked, tightening the lug nuts on the spare tire. "Are things over between you?"

She winced at the personal question. The hardest part had been knowing she'd hurt him. "I—"

"You know, forget I asked." Grant looked up at her, frowning. "That's none of my business."

"It's okay. He emailed me a dozen times the first couple months, convinced I'd just got cold feet and would be back. It was the hardest thing I ever did, because I truly loved him, but... I don't know. I was sitting across from him talking about the impact that fund-raiser had on me, and what I could do if I went, and I realized he didn't get it. And that's when I knew I couldn't marry him. We were at different places in our lives, and had different goals. He was on the fast track in a Fortune 500 company, and I realized that wasn't the life I wanted. I was tired of having everything and still feeling like something was missing."

"It must have been hard to let go of someone you'd planned to spend the rest of your life with."

Maddie caught the emotion in his voice as he finished securing the tire. "You sound as if you're speaking from experience."

"That's a whole other story."

"Try me," she said, wondering how she'd managed to find herself in the middle of nowhere, sharing her heart with a handsome superhero, who'd risked his life to save hers. Because in the process, despite the uncertainty of their situation, he'd managed to make her feel safe. Like nothing bad could happen as long as he was with her.

"Long story short, her name was Micah. I was planning to propose, but it never got that far. She couldn't handle my job, how much I traveled and the fact that every time I went out I was risking my life. She thought it was foolish and selfish of me. Told me that to my face. I don't know, maybe she was right."

"It's hard not to understand her fears."

Despite the attraction between them, she couldn't imagine a life with him. But neither could she stop herself from being drawn to his courage and lack of fear—a direct contrast to her struggle to control her own terror. She'd learned to mask it by slipping into her professional role, but she didn't know how to escape it. Not completely. And especially not today.

"I hope you know that whatever happens here, the risk you take every day with people like Ana…it's worth it." Silence hovered between them as he stood up and brushed off his hands.

"You about ready? I'll put the jack and flat tire away if you want to get Ana back in the car."

Maddie walked away from the car to where Antonio and Ana were sitting in the shade. Moving here had been worth it. But losing her heart to a man who took too many risks? That was an entirely different situation.

"Hey, sweetie." Maddie crouched beside Ana. "How are you feeling?"

"Antonio told me I could meet his twin daughters, Lucia and Julia."

"That sounds wonderful. Listen, the car's fixed, which means we can go now. And as soon as we get to the boat you can sleep, okay?"

Ana nodded as they helped her back into the car and made sure she had her seat belt on.

Antonio closed the door and turned back to Maddie. "How do you think she's doing?"

"Her fever's climbing again."

She didn't want to worry him, but she knew that not only did symptoms tend to come and go in cycles, they also could progress rapidly and become fatal within twenty-four hours if not treated. They needed to get to the mainland, where she would ensure Ana was cared for properly.

"But that's not all, is it?" he prodded.

"She's showing signs of jaundice."

"Which means?"

"She needs medical attention. If left untreated it can affect her brain, kidneys and lungs."

And not only was there nothing more she could do for Ana, they still had to find a way around the washed-out road and get to the ferry before they were found.

"Grant?"

She turned around when he didn't answer, then froze. A black mamba snake had reared up off the ground, inches away from where Grant stood.

EIGHT

Grant barely heard Maddie's voice above the pounding of his heart. An adult black mamba, at least six feet long, slithered in front of him. His neck pulsed as the snake reared two-thirds of its body up off the ground and stared him straight in the eyes.

Seconds ticked by in slow motion. Grant held his breath. Frozen.

He'd seen his share of snakes while removing land mines, but never a black mamba. Two drops of venom could kill a person. And without antivenom, one bite was enough to be a death sentence.

The gray-skinned snake spread its cobra-like neck flap, opened its mouth and hissed, then vanished into the bush as quickly as it had appeared.

Grant expelled the air out of his lungs.

"Grant?"

He turned around to where Maddie stood, his heart still racing. The encounter might have only lasted seconds, but those few seconds had felt like a lifetime. He wiped the perspiration off the back of his neck and drew in a long, slow breath. Why was it that he'd hovered over dozens of land mines and was used to the soar of adrenaline when potentially facing death, but somehow that snake had the power to send the chill of death through him?

"You okay?" Maddie asked.

"You saw that, didn't you?" he asked, shoving his hands into his pockets to stop them from shaking.

"Yes, and if I'd been standing where you are right now, I think I would have passed out from fright."

"Thankfully, it's gone," Antonio said, "though I have a feeling it was far more scared of you, than you were of it. They might be lethal, but they're also very skittish."

"He looked me in the eye," Grant said as he got into the car. "Man, I hate those things."

"Okay, I've got to ask you something," Maddie said as he started the engine and continued slowly through the rice fields, looking for a place to turn around on the other side of the gully. "You deactivate explosives for a living, but you hate snakes? Not that I blame you, by the way, but it just…I don't know…surprises me."

She might be right, but that didn't help alleviate the lingering panic still circulating through him. "I blame it on the time I was ten years old and went overnight camping with my grandfather in East Texas. When we started packing up the next morning, I pulled up my tent, and curled up beneath where my pillow had been was a sleeping cottonmouth. Far as I know, it had been there all night. It took months before he convinced me to go camping again. And, poisonous or not, every time I see a snake my skin crawls."

"Well, that thing *was* almost as tall as you are." Maddie pressed her lips together.

Grant glanced at her, not missing her attempt not to smile. "And now you're laughing at me."

"I'm not laughing."

"He could have bit me."

"But he didn't."

He shot her a smile. "I still say you're laughing."

"I'm really not," she said, "Though your face did turn a bit...chalky."

"You're not going to let me live this down, are you?"

"I did tell you what I would have done. You're far braver than I am, hands down."

He couldn't help but laugh. "If you say so."

Grant glanced at Maddie sitting beside him and realized it was more than just the encounter with the black mamba that had him feeling off balance. Because *cowardly* wasn't exactly a word he'd use to describe her. It had taken courage to leave her practice and family to work in a third-world country with a completely different culture.

And as far as he could tell, she didn't do it because of guilt.

So how had he managed to sweep in and rescue her when it felt like she was the one with the ability to rescue his heart? And while he was emotionally drawn to her sense of empathy and love for people, he knew there were other factors involved in his feelings toward Maddie. What he felt could be nothing more than one of those instances where an intense situation bonds two people more quickly than it would in real life. But once they got back to normal, the feelings no longer remained.

He'd seen it happen to a friend of his, Paul. Paul had met Lana the day Lana's brother died. Ivan, who'd been working for their organization as a trained deminer, accidentally hit a mine and triggered a fatal explosion.

Paul had rushed Ivan to the hospital and met Lana there. He'd visited her every day after her brother's funeral, and eventually fallen in love. Or so he'd thought. But it didn't take long for Paul to realize that their relationship had been built on the emotions of the situation and not on something solid.

The cell phone rang, pulling him away from his thoughts.

"It's the phone you bought in the market," Maddie said, grabbing it from the console between the seats and handing it to him.

Grant pressed the phone against his ear with his shoulder, and kept both hands on the wheel. "Colton?"

"Grant...can you hear me?"

Grant gave out a sigh of relief at his friend's voice. "The connection's pretty bad, but yes. Where are you? Are you okay?"

"Thanks to your text message, I got out of there. Saw the explosion from the air. But what about you?"

"Long story, but Antonio and I managed to get Maddie out of that camp this morning. We should be at the dock to catch the ferry to the mainland in about ten minutes, but they're looking for us."

"I know. That's why I've been trying to get ahold of you. I've got a contact on the ground who told me they're watching the two airstrips." There was a slight pause on the line. "That means I can't fly in, but there's still got to be something I can do. If nothing else, I can contact the American Embassy in Dakar and Maddie's aid organization. Her family's going to want to know she's okay."

"No—"

"No?"

Grant hesitated. While he appreciated his friend's offer, if someone in the State Department was behind this the last thing they needed to do was contact the embassy. Because beyond his tight circle of friends, he wasn't sure who they could trust. Even contacting Maddie's family could end up jeopardizing their lives if word got out.

"Listen." Grant shifted into to third and swung around a large ditch on the side of the road. "I can't explain everything now, but I need you to keep this quiet for the moment. Don't tell anyone you've spoken to me. It's not safe."

"What do you mean? If you rescued her, and she's okay—"

"There's more involved than just her kidnapping. Trust me, I'll explain everything once we get to Bissau, but for now I need you to keep this quiet."

"Okay, but there's got to be something I can do in the meantime."

"Meet us at the dock in Bissau when the ferry arrives. We're going to need a safe place to go and computer access."

"Of course. You've got it."

Grant hung up the phone as they finally made it to the outskirts of town, marked by more people along the sides of the roads. Wisps of smoke above the palm trees from cooking fires. The recent rain had made the streets muddy with pools of water.

"Colton will meet us on the mainland," he told her.

"If we make it to there."

"We will." He wanted so badly to reassure her that he'd protect her from whoever was out there, but what if he couldn't? "And as soon as we get to Bissau, we'll be able to see what's on this flash drive and hopefully put a stop to all of this."

"We're almost there," Antonio said. "The dock is just around the corner."

And if it had already left?

Grant stamped away the thought. He wasn't ready to deal with those consequences. Not unless they had to.

Grant let out a deep sigh of relief as the road curved and the rusty ferry came into view with crowds of people lining the dock. "It might not be our own private speedboat, but I don't think I've ever been quite so grateful to see one of these ferries."

The dock bustled with people as Maddie made her way behind Grant and toward the aging boat a few minutes later, holding on tightly to Ana's hand, while Antonio bought their tickets. Already passengers and cargo had filled up the edges of the deck, while others sat beneath the shelter on the top. She scanned the crowd, but so far there was no sign of the men who'd been after them.

"You're certain this is seaworthy," she asked, trying to keep the worry out of her voice.

"Let's hope so, because it's the safest transport we're going to find out of here."

Maddie frowned at Grant's response, but realized even he couldn't give her any guarantees. Because a boatload of people facing a storm wasn't the only thing that had her worried. She glanced behind them into the growing crowd that pressed against them, continuing to search for the men they'd seen earlier this morning. But here, even in a throng of people, there was no way they could hide. And if the men found them before they got on this ferry and left the port, there was nowhere else to run.

She grabbed on to Grant's arm and started praying as they continued through the throng of people, her other hand tight around Ana's fingers. She might have teased Grant over his black mamba encounter, but she understood his reaction all too well. Because she was facing her own mounting fears. Until they were back on the mainland she wasn't going to feel safe, and even there, this wasn't going to be over. They needed to know who was behind this. Needed to know what information Sam had died trying to get.

She watched as men off-loaded cargo from the ferry onto the dock. Fifty-kilogram bags of rice, fish, live chickens, half a dozen cows and a pile of foam mattresses. Someone dragged a squealing pig across the deck, while another man carried cashew wine in large motor oil containers. The pungent smell of the animals engulfed her, tempered only by the scent of rain in the air. She shifted her gaze out across the choppy water. The sky had turned even darker as the wind blew the churning clouds their direction. It wasn't going to be long until the brunt of the storm arrived.

Antonio maneuvered his way back through the crowd to where they stood. "I got some of the last seats in the only air-conditioned room. It was more expensive, but it will give Ana a place to sleep and will ensure we don't get drenched if and when the rains hit."

Maddie followed the men across wobbly wooden planks onto the boat. The humid breeze off the ocean wasn't enough to eliminate the stench of the livestock emanating from the crowded ferry. Still, she supposed, the situation could be worse. The boat appeared to be seaworthy—at least she hoped so.

Inside the enclosed "VIP" section, the room was full of padded benches, a TV blaring in the background and a front-row view of the sea. A couple dozen people had already settled into the unassigned seats, including the only other foreigner she'd seen boarding, who was settled in beside his heavy backpack with a pair of earphones.

"You can sleep again, sweetie." Maddie tried to get Ana settled onto one of the empty benches and checked her forehead with the back of her hand. Thankfully, the pain medicine she'd given her from the limited supplies she'd brought with her was finally beginning to work and her fever was down again. But a dose of acetaminophen wasn't going to fight against malaria. Only its symptoms.

Ana gave her a sleepy smile.

"A few more hours, and we'll be in Bissau where I can get you the medicine you need."

"And I can see my grandma?"

Maddie nodded. "We're going to do everything we can to find her. I promise."

The ferry was already leaving the dock by the time she went to sit beside Grant and Antonio, close enough that she'd be able to keep her eye on Ana. "Guess we just made it."

"How is she?" Antonio asked.

"Okay for now. The sooner we get to the mainland, the better. She still needs the proper medication, but rest and fluids will have to do for now."

She grabbed a bottle of water from her backpack,

took a long sip and then stopped herself from spewing a mouthful.

She held up her hand. "Okay, I'm sorry, but there are a couple of things mixed up here. Warm drinking water and cold showers."

She couldn't even remember the last time she'd taken a hot shower. Or had a glass of water—or anything for that matter—with ice. She forced another swallow and screwed the cap back on. Hopefully by tonight all of this would be over and she'd be enjoying a real shower and a hot meal.

"Trust me, I've thought the same thing a time or two." Grant laughed and caught her gaze. "What about breakfast? You haven't eaten yet, and there are still a couple boiled eggs."

Maddie frowned. Worry had squashed her appetite, and she was certain her stomach wasn't going to be able to handle a boiled egg this morning.

"Any cashews left?" She knew she should eat something.

Grant reached into his bag tossed her the rest of the nuts.

"Thanks." Maddie popped a cashew into her mouth and glanced out the glass window. They were finally moving away from the dock.

Just a few more hours, God. I just need You to get me through the next few hours.

"The two of you don't get seasick, do you?" Grant asked.

"On Tilt-A-Whirl, and anything that spins, really, but thankfully not on boats," Maddie said. "Of course, I've never been on a rusty ferry out in the middle of a storm. It's bound to get rough at some point."

"Let's just say I've always preferred solid ground, which is why I'm going to walk around for a while," Antonio said. "I need some fresh air."

"Do you think he's feeling seasick?" Maddie asked, as Antonio slipped out of the room.

"I have a feeling he wouldn't tell us even if he was."

Just like she had no desire to let on how scared she really was. All morning she'd tried to stop herself from going through all the possible scenarios of what could happen. Like what would happen if *they* were waiting on the mainland. What would happen if the storm worsened and the boat started to sink? And what would happen if her mother had to attend a second funeral of one of her children?

She tried to dismiss the negative thoughts. She'd always been the one in the family who saw the bright side of things and the glass half full. But now...after everything that had happened over the past few days, finding the bright side of anything was getting harder and harder to do.

"Tired?" Grant asked, leaning back beside her on the bench.

"Yeah." She rubbed her temples with her fingertips, trying to alleviate some of the tension. "I haven't slept much in days, and when I do close my eyes, I keep seeing Gavin's face staring up at me. That and thinking about what my mother has to be feeling right now."

"As soon as I know you're safe, we'll call her. And in the meantime, why don't you try to sleep?" he said. "It's going to be a few hours."

Despite the television blaring in the background, she had a feeling sleep would come quickly if she let it.

"You sure?" she asked.

"I promise to wake you up if Ana needs you, but right now she's asleep as well. And you're exhausted."

He wrapped his arm around her shoulder and pulled her against him. She could hear the beating of his heart. Steady. Solid. Constant. It was a place she wanted to stay. A place where she felt safe. And at the same time a dangerous place where she knew she could easily lose her own heart.

Grant had spent his life living in the middle of the action, because that was who he was. He was a soldier. A warrior. She'd simply come here to help people and in her small way make a difference. She would never be ready to sign on for a lifetime with someone like him, who risked his life every day. And neither could she even dream she could make him into something he wasn't.

The boat shuddered beneath them. The engines cut for a moment, slowed to a stop, then came back on again. She pushed the worry aside for the moment and breathed in the faint scent of peppermint candy and the woodsy scent of his shirt instead. She wanted—needed—to feel safe. And he had somehow managed to do that.

He brushed back her hair from her eyes and smiled down at her. "I wish I could make you promises that all of this will be over soon, but you know I can't do that. But we have gotten this far. And right now, at this moment, you're safe."

"I know."

She let herself settle into his arms and felt the stress that had latched on to her start to slip away. He was right. They had managed to escape and make it all the way to the crowded ferry. Ana's fever was down for the moment. And there was no way that the people who were after them could find them in the middle of the ocean. All they had to do now was make it to the mainland where his pilot friend was waiting. Then all of this would be over.

Unable to fight it anymore, she closed her eyes and fell asleep to the beating of Grant's heart.

Grant watched Maddie sleep. She was beautiful, of that there was no doubt, but his growing interest went beyond attraction. He'd never met a woman who held such a passion for people. Who was willing to give up everything she was familiar with to follow a deeper sense of calling. And they were alike in so many ways. His efforts went toward preventing future disasters. She was there when disaster struck.

He shook his head. *What's happening, Lord? Is it even possible to think that a relationship might have a chance to spark between us?*

Except he wasn't looking for a relationship. Despite the intense draw he felt toward Maddie, he knew it could never work. He lived on the edge, facing potential disaster each day. He'd learned the hard way that his life wasn't a life women wanted to share with him. Letting his gaze drift out across the now darkened waters, he frowned at the reality of his situation. How could he ever expect someone to agree to live with the relentless dangers his job entailed and the days and weeks he wouldn't be home?

He studied her dark hair with its flecks of red, and her lashes lying against her cheeks while she slept. The stress of the past few days that had been so evident in her expression seemed to have temporarily vanished.

It was strange how a week ago he'd been planning to go to a Broncos game with a couple of his friends, but now, for some crazy reason, he knew there was nowhere he'd rather be sitting than next to Maddie Gilbert, even if it was on a run-down ferry somewhere along the Atlantic coastline of one of the world's poorest countries.

Twenty minutes later, Antonio slipped back into the crowded room and sat down across from him.

"You don't look so good, are you feeling okay?" Grant asked.

"Remember the last time I had malaria?" Antonio coughed and let out a low groan. "If it's possible, I feel worse."

"Fever?" Grant asked.

"No. A weak stomach doesn't sound very macho, but I think it's just a nasty bout of seasickness."

Grant laughed. "At least you've still got your sense of humor. Did the fresh air help any?"

"Some." Antonio leaned forward and rested his arms against his thighs. Any traces of a smile had vanished. "But I think we might have even bigger problems."

Grant frowned. "You're kidding right?" The last thing they needed was another obstacle to getting them out of here.

"I wish. There's a speedboat out there on the water, and it's heading directly for this ferry."

NINE

They were coming for them.

Grant felt a wave of adrenaline shoot through him. He shouldn't be surprised. If those men were determined enough to find them, it was a logical assumption to search the ferry headed toward the mainland.

He glanced at Maddie, hating to wake her up if this was a false alarm. But experience had told him not to ignore his gut. He didn't think this could be just a coincidence.

"You think it's them," Grant said.

It was a statement at this point. Not a question.

Antonio nodded. "And you can take your pick of bad guys this time. Insurgents from the camp, or the local authorities."

Grant frowned at the confirmation as his mind tried to come up with a plan to get them to safety. But how did one escape from a run-down ferry in the middle of the ocean?

"Any suggestions if we're both right?" he asked. "There's no way we'll be able to hide."

"I know. I'm trying to find an answer to that same question."

Guilt seeped through Grant's gut. Deactivating land mines required that he stayed calm and focused in tense situations, but with Maddie and Ana in the equation the stakes had multiplied. An image of Darren flashed before him. While the odds might be against them, he had to find a way to put an end to this. But if these were the men who were after them, he had no idea how he was going to stop them.

"How long do we have until they reach the boat?" Grant asked, ignoring the noise from the television and conversation around the crowded VIP room.

Antonio leaned forward and lowered his voice. "Three…four minutes tops."

Grant's mind played through the obvious scenario. Security on a boat like this would be minimal. Which made two or more armed intruders, a boat full of passengers and a storm quickly pressing in a recipe for disaster.

The ferry jolted beneath them. Grant gripped Maddie's waist as she started to slide off the chair. His heart wanted to shield her from what was going on for as long as possible, but reality demanded something different. Because time was quickly running out and this wasn't something he could hide from her.

Her eyes fluttered opened. "What's going on?"

"That was just the boat's engines," he said, hoping to calm her. "But…"

"But what?" She sat up, fully awake now.

"Antonio just spotted a speedboat headed our way." Grant prayed silently for wisdom as he stood. "He and I need to get out there so we can find out who they are and figure out what to do. And I need you to stay here with Ana."

"Wait…no…" She glanced at Ana who still lay sleeping. Then she stood up beside him. "I'll come with you."

"Forget it," he said, already missing the warmth of her in his arms as he headed toward the window. The speedboat was coming in fast and still on course to intercept the ferry. "Antonio and I will go see who it is. And if we get lucky, it won't be anything to worry about."

"Nothing to worry about?" Maddie stopped beside him, the frown on her face telling him she didn't believe his optimism. "I need to come with you."

"Maddie—"

"If it's the men from the camp, I should be able to recognize them. You can't. And for all we know, they could be pirates. I can help you know who we're dealing with. And besides, if they are after me, what difference will it make? They'll find me in here just as easily as on the deck."

"Pirates?" Grant hesitated, but knew she had a point. While the waters off the coast of West Africa received far less attention than Somalia's dangerous coastline, attacks in West Africa's Gulf of Guinea were becoming more and more frequent.

"I don't know." Grant stared out the window. "Pirates are going to attack offshore oil facilities or cargo vessels. Not a ferry filled with local passengers."

"Maybe. But you still need me." Fear laced her expression, but he didn't miss the determination coupled with it. "And we don't have time to argue. I'll have the lady we were sitting next to look after Ana."

"Fine, but stay behind me." Grant grabbed Maddie's hand as soon as she'd seen to Ana's care, and they hurried toward the steps leading to the lower deck where there was a row of cars parked. "I'll stay with you behind one of these cars, where you can see, but at least you'll have some protection. Antonio, I'm assuming the captain's already seen the boat, but he might need a heads-up of what this could turn into."

"I'll try to find him," Antonio said.

Gusty winds blew against Grant's face as the three of them stepped onto the deck of the crowded ferry. He and Maddie hurried toward an old Land Rover for cover. Thirty seconds later, three men boarded the side of the boat, yelling instructions at the passengers, their weapons raised.

"Do you recognize any of them?" Grant asked her from their partially protected vantage point.

Shots filled the air before she had a chance to answer. Passengers screamed. Grant pulled Maddie onto the deck floor and covered her with his body. Her muscles flinched beneath him as a second round of gunfire discharged above them.

The spray of bullets exploded into the air. Maddie's back slammed against the deck. Opening her eyes, she saw Grant's face hovering inches above hers, his blue eyes peering straight through her.

"Are you all right?" he asked.

The shooting stopped, unlike the rapid pounding of her heart. She looked away, willing her pulse to slow down. "I think so."

He grabbed her hand and helped her to her feet, making sure she stayed hidden beside the vehicle. She scanned the deck from her position to where the men stood on a platform near the railing of the ferry, guns pointed as they yelled at the passengers.

"Two of them are from the camp," she whispered. "The one with the scar on his cheek and the tall skinny one. I don't recognize the third."

"Can you understand what they're saying?"

"Yeah. They're looking for two foreigners," she said translating their Portuguese.

"I'm guessing that's us," Grant said, his voice laced with sarcasm.

Maddie's stomach clenched. With no escape off the boat, and nowhere to hide, no matter what they did, this wasn't going to end well. They'd killed Sam and Gavin. She was going to be next.

Still shouting at the passengers, one of the men stepped into the crowd, heading toward their location.

"Where's he going?" Grant asked, pulling her back into the shadows.

She shook her head. "I don't know."

If he'd seen them…

Familiar feelings of panic swept through her. The same panic she'd felt the day she'd watched them shoot Gavin. The same terror she'd felt when they kidnapped her, knowing she'd be dead as soon as they didn't need her anymore.

The man stopped in the middle of the crowd and grabbed someone. Seconds later they emerged to where she could see them again. Maddie's heart plummeted.

Antonio.

She pressed her hand against her mouth, fear continuing to spread through her. "They recognized him."

The man with the scar across his cheek aimed his weapon at Antonio's chest. "Where are the other two?"

Antonio looked him in the eye. "I don't know."

"And *I* don't believe you. If you want to live, tell me

where your friends are. Otherwise I will shoot you, and we'll still find them." He let out a hollow laugh. "It's not as if they have anywhere to go."

Maddie grabbed Grant's arm. It was too late to save themselves. They were out of options. These men had killed before and clearly negotiating wasn't an option. Which meant the only chance of saving Antonio was to give them what they wanted.

"What do you want from them?" Antonio asked.

"We have orders to finish a botched job."

Maddie's gaze automatically dropped to the flash drive. "The day they shot Gavin…they must have had orders to kill me. I was the one they were after."

"But someone decided to take you instead of killing you because of the medical crisis." Grant caught her gaze. "They must still believe you know something, but they probably don't realize that Sam gave you a drive that holds the information. Because if they did, they would have already taken it."

She shook her head. "And now I can't let them hurt you or Antonio. You never should have come, Grant."

Grant squeezed her hand. "It's too late for that, Maddie. Antonio and I both knew what we were getting into when we got on that plane."

"No, you didn't—"

"Wait." Grant grabbed her arm as she started to move. "You're not going out there. If you can slip around to the other side of the ferry and get onto their speedboat—"

"Forget it. That would be suicide for you and Antonio, and they'd stop me with their weapons."

"Maddie."

Her eyes filled with tears. "No matter what we do, they

will find us—all of us—and you know that. This is the only way. If nothing else, maybe they'll let Antonio go."

Maddie pulled away from Grant and made her way through the crowded deck, her legs threatening to give out beneath her.

There has to be a way out of this, God. Please.

She couldn't watch another person she cared about die. And now that she'd made the decision there was no turning back.

She felt Grant's fingers slip around her hand and pull her toward him. "Then we do this together."

She nodded, allowing his touch to give her a boost of courage. But, whatever had motivated him, whatever was driving him, he never should have come.

Grant stepped out in front of her and then stopped, his hands held up. "Let him go. We're the ones you're looking for."

"Ah… Dr. Gilbert. I thought this might motivate you. Clearly Oumar's men made a mistake, keeping you alive the first time."

"So you're going to, what…shoot us in front of all of these people?" Maddie asked.

"Not yet. There's someone who needs to talk to you first. Which is why you're both coming with me."

"Not so fast." A loud voice shouted from the upper deck of the ferry. "This is the captain. I want the three of you to put your weapons down. Now."

The man with the scar grabbed Maddie and shoved his gun against her head. "I don't think so."

"Wait…please—" Grant said as another man pulled him back.

"Shut up!"

She winced as he pressed the metal barrel harder

into her skull. The crowd fell silent around them, leaving only the sound of the engine and the lapping waves against the sides of the ferry. She caught Grant's gaze, but there was nothing left to do.

"Here's what's going to happen." Her captor's other hand squeezed her arm. "They're coming with me. All three of them."

"Let them go," Maddie said.

"Maddie—" Grant began.

"They don't know what Sam told me," she continued. "That's why you want me dead, isn't it?"

"You're a smart girl, but—"

"Apparently you didn't hear what I said," the captain shouted. "I said put your weapons down."

"I don't think so."

"Really? Because if you harm anyone of these passengers, you and your friends won't make it off the boat alive."

Maddie heard the cocking of a rifle and glanced up. Four men—in addition to the captain—stood at strategic locations around the ferry, their weapons aimed at the three men.

"You think I don't know who you are?" The captain shouted. "You flash your weapons and money and power around, but not on my boat. And definitely not on my watch."

The engines jolted and the deck shifted beneath them. Maddie stumbled as a shot rang out. The man next to Grant dropped to the deck. Using the distraction to her advantage, she pulled away from her captor and ran into the crowd.

Grant, Antonio and a couple of the passengers quickly disarmed the men. In a matter of seconds, the three men were lying facedown on the deck. The crowd cheered, but Maddie couldn't breathe. Instead, a wave of nausea flooded through her. The deck swayed beneath her. She felt Grant's arms surround her, holding her up, but she couldn't stop shaking. Couldn't stop thinking about what had almost happened.

"It's over, Maddie. It's over."

"Tie them up." The captain ordered as he stepped up beside them. "As long as you're on my boat, they won't be able to hurt you."

The captain had come down onto the deck, and Grant reached out to shake his hand, his other arm still wrapped around Maddie's waist. "You took a risk to save our lives."

The captain nodded, his dark skin glistening from the high humidity of the approaching storm. "And I'd do it again. This was personal."

"Why?" Maddie's voice cracked.

"These men—along with dozens of others—get rich from the cocaine that passes through these islands. But not everyone in my country supports the drug trade. Most of my brothers are fishermen like my father, but so much has changed." The older man folded his arms across his chest and hesitated. "My daughter and a friend found these packages of white powder on the shoreline. They thought it was something to season their food. That night seven people in my family became sick. My daughter died from an overdose of cocaine. She was ten years old."

Maddie felt her breath catch. "I'm so sorry."

"So am I."

Maddie watched the captain walk away while his

BUSINESS REPLY MAIL
FIRST-CLASS MAIL   PERMIT NO. 717   BUFFALO, NY

POSTAGE WILL BE PAID BY ADDRESSEE

READER SERVICE
PO BOX 1867
BUFFALO NY 14240-9952

NO POSTAGE
NECESSARY
IF MAILED
IN THE
UNITED STATES

deckhands finished tying up the men. "I need to go check on Ana."

"I'll come with you," Grant said.

The man with the scar on his face sat on the corner of the deck, his hands secured behind him.

"Just because you stopped us now, doesn't mean this is over," he shouted. "There are others, and they will find you."

Maddie stopped midstride and turned around.

"Don't listen to them," Grant said, pressing her forward.

"Why not?" She looked back up at him and caught his gaze, the knot in her stomach refusing to loosen. "They're right. When we get to the capital, others will be there waiting for us. Because we might have survived today, but this is far from over."

TEN

Grant looked out one of the windows in the VIP section, staring at the gray waters while Maddie made up a new batch of rehydration drink across the room. He wondered how much progress they'd actually made toward the mainland. And while he was thankful they were still alive, all he could see was miles of the ghostly sea—with no signs of any of the surrounding islands.

"Maddie was right about this not being over." Antonio said, stepping up beside him. "You've noticed how the engine keeps stopping and starting."

"Yes?" Grant wasn't sure he liked where the conversation was going.

"Apparently the captain is having engine trouble, though no one is really saying what's going on. Rumors are that there's water in the oil. But whatever the problem, the fact that the engine keeps cutting out speaks volumes."

"So what do we do?" Grant asked.

"There's nothing we can do. Not at the moment, anyway."

Grant frowned, but knew his friend was right. While his first response was always to fix things, he'd learned that forcing things to happen didn't always work on this side of the world.

"How's Maddie doing? Antonio asked.

Grant glanced across the room where she sat beside Ana. "The encounter with those men really shook her up, but she's strong. A lot stronger than even she thinks."

He'd been impressed by her fortitude, especially when her own life had been at risk. Instead of running, she'd shown incredible courage. Something that made him want to get to know her even more.

"She's also perfect for you."

Grant looked at Antonio, surprised by his bluntness. Maybe he'd rubbed off too much on his friend. "Maddie?"

"Don't act all surprised," Antonio said. "You don't think I haven't noticed the way you look at her, and the way she looks back? The two of you have this connection. And if you ask me, she's exactly what you need."

"I don't know." He tried to shrug off the comment. "It's been years since I saw her, and to me she's always been my best friend's little sister. Friends only."

And besides, just because he was attracted to her didn't change the choices he'd made in life. Family and a wife weren't exactly on the radar.

"Well, just in case you didn't notice," Antonio said. "His little sister's all grown up."

Grant smiled. "Oh, trust me, I've noticed, but I came to keep a promise to her brother. Nothing more."

"So? What woman doesn't dream of some hero coming to their rescue?" Antonio leaned back and folded his arms across his chest. "The problem is that, while you might have rescued her, you're far too stubborn to see the possibilities outside your little world. Remember the last time my wife invited you over for dinner?"

Grant's brow rose, uncertain as to where his friend was going with his question. "I remember she made my favorite chicken dish with onions and lemon."

"It's called yassa." Antonio chuckled. "I also remember she said it was about time you found yourself a wife."

"I'm not looking for a wife."

"Why? Because one girl broke your heart?"

"No, because…" Grant let out a slow groan, wondering who he was trying to convince. Himself or Antonio. "Let's just face it. I don't exactly have a typical nine-to-five job. I spend most of my time traveling, and when I'm out in the field, I work with explosives. Most women don't like the thought of their boyfriend or husband dying while out trying to deactivate a land mine."

"Then get a different job. With your experience, you could teach, work in demolition, become a bomb expert for one of your local police departments… I don't know, but what I do know is that settling down with a good woman is a good thing. And worth it. It's time you got married and had a couple kids. It will quickly show you what's important in life. Things like family."

Antonio made changing career paths sound as simple as going to the store and switching to a different brand of deodorant.

"You make it sound so easy," Grant said.

"Maybe it's easier than you think."

But family had never been straightforward as far as he was concerned.

"Listen," Antonio continued. "I know you're not close to your own family. That's why I'm sticking my nose in your business. Because it's something you don't have, maybe you don't really know what you're missing. I'm telling you, it's worth it."

Grant looked down at Maddie again and felt that familiar ache run through him. If he let himself, he could almost imagine settling down. With her. But Antonio had been right about his own family. His mother had died when he was thirteen, and his and his father's relationship had been anything but smooth over the years. When they were together, they fought. When they were apart, it was easy to simply ignore each other. It didn't make for enjoyable Thanksgiving dinners or memorable Christmases around the tree.

A stepmother thrown into the picture when he was seventeen hadn't helped, either. She'd been critical toward him and jealous of his father's time. Not that he'd been the perfect stepson. An aunt had tried to help by stepping in and offering a place for him to stay when his stepmom wanted to kick him out. Instead he'd signed up for the military.

It had turned out to be the best decision he'd ever made. He might not have a family to go home to during the holidays, but friends like Darren and Antonio, along with his church family back home, had more than made up for it. Even so, he'd all but given up on the idea of having his own family one day.

"How's your nausea?" Grant asked, needing to change the subject. "I could ask Maddie if she has something that might help."

"You're good at avoiding issues you don't want to deal with."

He shot his friend a smile. "And you're good at butting into other people's business."

"But I'm right, aren't I?"

* * *

Maddie's rib cage pressed against her lungs as the boat shuddered beneath them. She handed Ana some of the new batch of the rehydration drink she'd just made. The men had been right. There were others out there. Looking for her. Wanting her dead. She sucked in a breath of air. When she was eight, her mother's bedtime stories had been enough to soothe any fears of monsters under the bed. At twenty-seven her mother was a continent away, and the monsters surrounding her wanted to kill her. If she stayed where she was, they would find her. Which was why all she wanted to do was run.

She glanced around the room at the padded benches. The television blared. Passengers dozed. A dark sea surrounded them. The boat lurched again and then shuddered to a halt.

"How are you doing?" Grant asked, walking up to her.

She smoothed back the loose wisps from her ponytail and looked out the window. They were surrounded completely by the sea, and the boat had stopped. "Why aren't we moving?"

"Apparently there's an issue with the engine," Grant said. "We've been stopping and starting for the past forty-five minutes. Antonio heard someone mention water in the engine oil."

"Water in the engine oil?" Maddie stood and walked across the room, still trying to wake up. Rain slashed against the windows. Lightning struck in the distance. "My stepfather used to tell me if it looks like someone poured a chocolate milkshake in your engine, there's probably water in the engine oil."

"Is it an easy fix?" Antonio asked.

"Depends. But it basically means we're broken down

in the Atlantic with a storm pounding around us until they find a solution." Maddie turned to Grant. "What about the phone you bought? Can't we... I don't know... call in the cavalry?"

"I thought of that," Grant said, "but the signal is worse here than it was on the island. And even if we had service, I'm not sure who to call. There isn't exactly a coast guard waiting to come to our rescue."

Maddie stared out the window, frowning as the reality of his words sank in. Even without the three men who'd showed up on the speedboat, the situation was precarious. Passengers who'd been milling along the deck when they first arrived were now huddled beneath the limited shelter, while the cargo on the main deck was caught in the downpour. And in their cooler, air-conditioned cabin, several, including the backpacker she'd noticed when they first sat down, seemed restless. But if Grant was right and it was someone from the State Department involved in her abduction, even if they could make a phone call, they couldn't go to the embassy for help.

Grant walked up beside her and nudged her with his shoulder. "A broken-down engine can be fixed."

"I know."

Her hand reached up automatically to finger the locket still hanging around her neck. Even if they fixed the engine, there were still men out there who wanted her dead. Her thoughts shifted to Ana, who had somehow managed to fall back asleep despite the constant buzz of conversation in the room and the rumbles of the boat beneath them. Maddie wasn't the only one at risk. They needed to get Ana to the mainland for medical help.

The backpacker stepped up next to them. "I over-heard you say something about the engines being down?" he asked in a strong British accent.

"We haven't heard anything official," Grant said, "but that's the rumor going around the boat."

"It's like the world's gone barmy." The stranger let out a sigh and combed his fingers through his longish blond hair. "Had a friend warn me about coming here. Told me it was the most beautiful undiscovered piece of paradise I'd ever see, but at the same time, the place had the potential to knock a person silly. After a bout with malaria, the constant rain and those armed men boarding the ship, I'm finally beginning to see what he meant. Though let me tell you, I still wouldn't have missed coming here for anything." He held out his hand. "Name's Alistair Hunter, by the way. I'm a photographer from the UK, here to do a photo shoot of Guinea-Bissau and the surrounding islands."

"Nice to meet you." Grant shook the man's hand. "I'm Grant Reese, and this is Maddie Gilbert and Antonio Balde. How long have you been traveling?"

"I was on the islands for about ten days. It was fantastic, but I decided that's about as long as I want to go with zero communication with the outside world save one hotel I stayed in. They have high-speed internet, but due to the heavy rains it wasn't quite fast enough to let me download my emails. And while the news ran 24/7, it was on an ancient television hanging on the wall off the lobby."

Maddie didn't miss the fact that Grant didn't give the man any specifics on who they were or why they were here. Which in her opinion was okay. There was no use getting someone else involved. Or putting anyone else's life on the line. Because more than likely, with the lack of internet, he had no idea who they were.

"I've got a travel cribbage board if any of you decide you need a distraction," Alistair said. "I've had fun teaching some of the locals how to play a favorite English pub game."

"Thanks," Grant said, clearly not wanting to offend him. "Maybe later."

Alistair nodded and headed back across the room. As far as Maddie was concerned though, even a riveting game of cribbage wasn't going to be able to distract her from what was going on.

"I need to check on Ana," Maddie said, noticing the young girl was stirring.

Maddie pressed her fingers gently against Ana's forehead, not wanting to wake her up as she settled back down at Maddie's touch.

"Is her fever down?" Grant asked.

"A little bit." Maddie pulled off her jacket and laid it on top of her backpack. Even with the air-conditioning running, the room still felt muggy. "Sleep is exactly what she needs right now."

"How about another patient, then?" Grant said. "Antonio's struggling with seasickness. I was wondering if you had anything that might help."

Maddie glanced at Antonio who'd crossed the room to join them. "You should have woken me up sooner."

"I told him there was nothing you could do," Antonio countered. "And I knew you needed your sleep."

"I'm a doctor." She shot him a grin. "I'm used to little sleep, but unfortunately, I don't have anything to give you specifically for motion sickness. If we had crackers, or apple juice or…" She looked at Grant.

"What?" he asked.

"Peppermints. I smelled them earlier. You have peppermints."

He looked to Antonio and then back to her. "So?"

"Peppermint oil can help ease the symptoms."

Grant dug around in the front pocket of his backpack and pulled out a handful of the red-and-white candy.

"Perfect. It's not Dramamine, but it might help some." She checked the water level in their water bottles and handed one to Antonio. Hopefully, they wouldn't run out before they docked. "You also need to drink as much as possible, Antonio. In fact, all of us do. With the humidity, it won't take long to get dehydrated. I'd also suggest you get out of this stuffy cabin and get some fresh air."

Antonio took a handful of peppermints from Grant. "The fresh air did help the last time, and it looks like the rain is letting up some. Besides that, maybe I can get some answers from the captain as to what's going on."

Maddie watched as he headed outside. Then she sat down beside Grant on the bench, leaving a space between them. Around them passengers dozed or listened to music on their earphones, seemingly unconcerned they weren't going anywhere. "It's funny, the things I remember. Like the fact that you loved peppermint candies."

"They were perfect to travel with when my sweet tooth acted up, because they didn't melt in places like this. My aunt used to send them to me wherever I was working. I got in the habit of carrying some in my backpack."

A stream of memories washed over her. Grant sitting next to her at the Thanksgiving dinner table. Watching football with the guys in the family room. Skiing together one winter in Aspen, while she was trying to figure out why he intimidated her almost as much as her first stint in ER. Because Grant had been unlike most guys she knew. Daring. Valiant. Fearless.

"You also loved my mom's Mississippi mud pie," she said,

"Oh, don't even go there. That's hardly fair when we're stuck here with nothing more than a few boiled eggs and a handful of cashews."

"And peppermint candies." Maddie laughed, welcoming the temporary distraction from their situation. "But yeah…my mom's cooking is great. She's always been a bit of a *Food Network* junkie. Always trying out new dishes."

"What else do you remember about me?" he asked, handing her a peppermint.

She pulled off the wrapper and popped the candy into her mouth. She couldn't exactly tell him how she remembered having a crush on him all those years ago. About how she'd always looked for an excuse to hang out with him and Darren. As far as she'd known, though, he'd never even really noticed her. She's simply been Darren's younger sister. And after Darren's death, he'd eventually stopped coming around.

"Because I remember you always asked Darren to bring you Lindt truffles and Toblerone whenever we were flying back through Europe," he said.

Maddie smiled. "I love that stuff. He always teased me because I couldn't make it last."

"That was because the few care packages we did get, we learned to ration out as long as possible."

She studied his profile, unable to deny the welcome

wave of comfort that enveloped her over the simple familiarity of his presence. Or the magnetism of those blue eyes and the dark shadow along his jawline. Their gazes locked briefly, making her wish Antonio would return. Because even all these years later, Grant still managed to leave her breathless.

She leaned forward and rested her elbows against her knees. "You keep asking me questions. Now it's my turn."

There was a hint of amusement in his eyes. "Okay. Shoot."

"What motivates you to risk your life?"

"You're getting serious on me." Grant shot her a smile. "All I can say is that after seven years in the military and a medical discharge, it seemed like a good career move."

Her eyes widened, though she shouldn't be surprised. Her brother had once told her the same thing. "So demining was simply a good career move?"

"Most of the time I'm simply involved in training locals to do the actual demining. I supervise their work and ensure cleared areas are marked properly." He clasped his hands together in front of him. "But yeah, I admit that most people tend to look at me like I'm some insane humanitarian. Someone who could get blown up trying to save the population of countries most people have never even heard of."

"And what do you tell them?"

"That it's the best way I've found to use my training to help others. And that there's no one waiting for me at home."

"Waiting to see if you'll come home, you mean. Alive

or in a coffin." *Like Darren.* Maddie looked away. "I'm sorry, but...don't you have plans to marry someday?"

She knew she'd crossed the line and that her questions were far too personal.

"I suppose when the right woman comes along I'll have to rethink things," he said. "What about you? Do you still think about marrying one day and having a family?"

She blushed under his steady gaze, but she'd walked herself right into this one.

"I do, actually." She flicked an invisible speck of lint off her pants and stared across the room, avoiding his gaze.

Movement caught her attention then. Alistair was pulling a laptop out of his backpack. She clutched the locket between her fingers, her adrenaline quickening. With a computer they could find out what was on the flash drive. But was it worth the risk?

ELEVEN

"We got us a computer." Grant grinned a minute later as he sat down beside Maddie and balanced the borrowed lightweight laptop on his knees.

"And our new friend over there didn't mind?" Maddie leaned toward Grant so she could see the screen.

"He said he could listen to music just as well as play games on this. We're going to have to hurry, though. Apparently there isn't much battery left."

Maddie flipped open the locket and handed him the flash drive.

Grant slid it into the USB port and clicked it open. "Wait a minute…it wants a password."

"A password?"

A safeguard box had popped up, verifying that the drive was locked with a password. "Did Sam give you one?"

Maddie shook her head. "No. He never mentioned a password."

He caught the concern in Maddie's voice and blew out a sigh of frustration. So far he felt as if they were fighting a phantom at every turn. If he was going to keep her safe, he needed to know what they were up against. And at the moment that meant they needed that password.

"Think, Maddie. Start going through your conversation with him again. There has to be a way to open this flash drive."

He started typing random words into the password box. *State Department... Guinea-Bissau... Drug Trafficking...*

Nothing.

"Wait a minute." Maddie rested her hand against his arm.

Grant looked up from the computer. "What is it?"

"Try Crystal."

"Okay. Why?"

"I hadn't been able to remember before, but her name was Crystal."

"Whose name?" Grant typed in the name.

"Remember I told you I thought he was talking about his girlfriend? What if Crystal's not a person, but a password?"

"You're right. We're in." Grant grinned as the list of documents popped up. "Not a bad password. Cocaine comes in two main forms, powder—"

"And a crystal rock form," Maddie finished.

"Okay, let's see what we've got on here." He started clicking through the documents. "The last file Sam opened was the day before his death. Looks like we've got a name... Reid Johnson. There's a pretty extensive profile of the guy."

"Who is he?" Maddie asked.

"I'm not sure yet." Grant skimmed through the document. "Born and raised outside of Detroit... Graduated from Liberty High School. Attended the University of

Michigan where he earned a degree in political science... This has got to be our guy. Look at this." Grant pointed at the screen. "He's worked with Homeland Security, congress, education and training initiatives, a post in DC, Country Director for West Africa, international security affairs..."

"And currently?"

"He works for the State Department and is connected to the US Embassy in Dakar." He let out a low whistle. "If this is right, Maddie, this guy's going to have a lot of clout."

"Enough clout to try to make sure I disappear."

"Unfortunately, yeah." He caught the fear in her voice and squeezed her hand. "But he's not going to win this. And now that we at least know who we're up against, I'm hoping we can somehow figure a way to be better prepared."

"What else is in there?"

Grant clicked open a dozen files and let them pop up across the desktop. The laptop's battery indicator showed it was almost at its end. "Look at this. It looks like Sam somehow got ahold of all the dirty details of this guy's secret life. Dozens of documents, spreadsheets, cell phone records of calls placed and received, off-shore bank account records and even emails all proving his involvement."

"Do you think he's the only one from the State Department who's involved?"

"I don't know."

Maddie leaned back against the bench and sighed. "What we do know is that Sam died for this information, Grant."

The thought was sobering. It also expelled any lingering question that Maddie had become a target because of Sam and the information they thought he'd passed on to her. Someone—namely Reid Johnson—couldn't afford for this information to get out. Grant started closing down all the files before the computer shut off. "Did Sam tell you where he got all of this?"

Maddie shook her head. "I wish he would have, but no."

Grant rubbed the back of his neck, waited for the computer to shut down. "To get this kind of information, someone had to have access to Reid's private files and records, and we can assume it wasn't on his work computer."

"It would have to have been someone close to him."

"Exactly. A secretary, colleague, girlfriend or some other close friend… Someone who found out his secret."

"Someone willing to betray him," she said.

Grant pulled out the flash drive, set it in her palm and closed her fingers around it. "There's a good chance Reid knows he's been betrayed. Maybe he doesn't know who betrayed him, but he clearly believed Sam was involved."

"Which was why he was willing to kill Sam to keep him quiet."

Grant tightened his fingers around hers, as the entire picture of what was going on became clear. "You're the link, Maddie. The last person to see Sam alive. And the only link between Sam and whoever gave him this information."

"But I have no idea who Sam talked to."

"Yes, but Reid doesn't know that. He's making assumptions while desperately trying to cover his tracks."

She slid the flash drive back into the locket. "Which

is why I'm scared, Grant. In spite of all my training in dealing with disasters, I've never been this close to death. It's like we're suspended in time, waiting for some horrible end to it all."

He reached down and wiped a tear that was running down her cheek. "Don't give up yet. Somewhere deep inside, I have to believe this is going to turn out all right."

She nodded, but he still caught the hesitation in her eyes.

He reached out and laced their fingers together. "We have the advantage now, Maddie. We know who he is."

"And no way to do anything about it."

"But we will. As soon as we reach the capital." He squeezed her hand. "In the meantime, I'll give the computer back to Alistair. Then I probably should go out and see if I can find Antonio. See if he's feeling any better."

She nodded.

Grant got up to return the computer, wishing there was something he could do with the information they'd just found. No cell phone communication. No internet access. Until the ferry docked their hands were completely tied.

Alistair was pulling out a digital camera from his backpack.

"Really appreciate you letting us borrow this," Grant said, handing him the computer.

"No problem." He slipped the computer into a padded section and held up his camera. "Thought I'd go take a few photos out on the deck. At least I'll end up with an interesting write-up with photos for the readers of my travel blog."

Alistair headed for the open deck while Grant made

his way back to his seat. He found Ana sitting up and sipping on some of Maddie's rehydration drink.

Grant crouched down next to the sleepy-eyed girl. "Morning, Ana. It's good to see you up and awake. How are you feeling?"

Ana gave him a weak smile. "Better."

"I'm glad to hear that," he said, standing back up.

A sudden jolt of the boat almost knocked Grant off his feet. Someone across the room screamed. He caught Ana with one arm and the edge of a bench with his hand, and managed to hold them both steady.

He quickly glanced around the room. Except for startled looks on a number of the passengers, no one looked hurt.

"Are you okay, Ana?" he asked.

She nodded while Maddie hurried to clean up Ana's spilled drink. "This is getting ridiculous."

"Yes, it is." Grant glanced toward the windows. The storm seemed to be dissipating, but the air conditioner had gone off, leaving the room stuffy with the humidity. "On the bright side, it does look like we're moving now."

"But for how long?"

A loud commotion toward the stern stopped Grant from attempting to answer her question. Someone screamed again. Shouting from below escalated. Most of the passengers in the VIP room headed to the windows to see what was happening.

Grant started toward the deck, just as Antonio stepped inside the room.

"Antonio...what's going on?"

"No one seems to know for sure. It looks like the ferry just hit something—a reef or a sandbar—but the bottom line is we're taking on water."

* * *

A drop of perspiration blurred Maddie's vision. She wiped her eyes with the back of her hand, fighting to process Antonio's words. And fighting to stop the panic sifting through her. Because the ferry couldn't be sinking. Not after everything else that had happened this past week. Not when they were so close to finally reaching the mainland.

"How serious a situation are we talking about at this point?" Grant asked.

"I'm not sure, but we need to prepare for the worst," Antonio said.

Maddie frowned. Two months ago, a local boat transporting people had sunk less than a mile off the coast. The majority of the fifty passengers had drowned. She tried to shake off the thought. She knew there wasn't time to wallow in what-ifs. Bracing her legs against the rocking of the craft, she looked out across the bewildered scurry of passengers on the deck below them. Men threw heavy bags of peanuts and other items overboard in an attempt to save the boat from sinking.

God, we need You to intervene in this situation. Please, God...

Maddie paused at the request. Growing up, praying had always been automatic whenever she needed something. But moving to Africa had slowly shifted the focus of her prayers almost entirely to her patients. Because somehow her own requests—at least compared to the situations she saw daily in the hospital—seemed frivolous. Not that God hadn't listened. Or didn't care. But she'd begun to realize just how much she really had. This past week, though, her prayers had shifted again, because never before had she faced the frightening reality of someone wanting to take her life. Or of the chain of events that had brought them to this moment.

"What's the captain doing?" Grant asked.

"They're trying to pump out the water and have radioed the capital for help. But even with the storm slowly dying out, there's no coast guard available to come to our rescue."

Maddie bit the edge of her lip. "We're also sitting ducks out here. What if whoever sent those men to grab us gets suspicious, and they send out more reinforcements?"

"Then we deal with that when—and if—it happens." Grant reached out and squeezed her hand. "The captain assured me that they are keeping an eye out for any oncoming vessels. I don't know what else we can do at this point."

Passengers darted across the deck. People shouted. Maddie worked to push away the fear as her brain kicked into emergency mode. Countless shifts in the ER had trained her to think clearly during a crisis and not give in to the spreading alarm that surrounded her. Because Grant was right. All they could do was focus on one crisis at a time. And for now, they were far enough out to sea that if something wasn't done quickly, their already difficult journey could quickly end in disaster. She had to do whatever she could to prepare.

She grabbed one of the bright orange life jackets that had been tucked away in case of an emergency, slipped it on over her head and secured the straps, before grabbing one for Ana.

She nodded at Grant. "The two of you need to put on a life jacket, along with everyone else."

They were pretty much completely off the grid, and

with no instructions on what to do in case of an emergency, she couldn't assume that the crew was fully prepared to manage a disaster without outside help.

"What do you know about boats?" she asked, slipping the old-fashioned life jacket over Ana's head. "How fast before something this size sinks?"

"There's no way to know, though a hole doesn't automatically mean a ship's going to sink. I don't know about this one, but many boats—whether large ferries or cruise ships—are compartmentalized like an ice cube tray," Grant said, after tossing a life vest to Antonio.

"Meaning if there's a hole, it will be limited to that section of the ship."

"Exactly. But a ship can only withstand so much flooding in any compartment before it sinks." Grant finished securing his life jacket. Then he and Antonio started handing out vests to the rest of the passengers still in the VIP room. "It's also possible that with the large swells, the cargo could have shifted, changing the center of gravity." He glanced toward the window. "There's an island over there," he said while pointing. "If the ferry does go down, it's the best option at this point."

"The only problem with that scenario…" Maddie said, pulling out another stack of life jackets from the open cupboard, "Despite living near the water, I've found that most people can't swim. Especially this far out from land."

"She's right." Antonio said in English, helping a young mother secure one of the life jackets around her waist alongside a couple of the crew members. "If this ferry goes down, this boat is going to turn into a graveyard."

Maddie kept praying as the helplessness of the situation swept through her. She didn't even want to think about worst-case scenarios, which were much more likely if the boat did sink. Instead she grabbed her medical bag, wondering if it was going to be enough.

"What about you, Antonio? How are you feeling?" Maddie grabbed Ana's hand and headed for the door, noticing that for the first time since they'd left the port his skin didn't look clammy.

"I'm still queasy, but those peppermints helped." Antonio adjusted the straps on his life jacket. "The fresh air helps a bit as well."

Maddie started walking again, but there was another question that had been nagging at her.

"What happened to the men on the speedboat?" she asked. "Did the captain move them?"

Grant looked to Antonio and then back at Maddie.

The uneasiness was back. "Tell me what happened."

"Antonio wanted to question them and asked the captain the same thing." Grant drew in a deep breath. "The captain killed them and dumped their bodies overboard. Apparently it really was personal for him."

Maddie stopped in the doorway, feeling the air rush out of her lungs. This time a sick feeling replaced the fear.

Oh, Lord. How did it come to this? Lives ruined on both sides because of revenge and greed.

The men deserved to be punished, but not this way. "Why would he do that?" she asked.

"Sometimes taking the law into your own hands is the only way to get justice in this part of the world," Antonio answered.

"But that doesn't make it right."

A loud hammering sounded from the engine of the boat. Then nothing.

"No, it doesn't," Grant said. "But for the moment we have other things to worry about. Sounds like they're having problems getting the engines going again. If we could just get close to that island…"

Halfway down the stairs, the boat lurched again. Maddie grabbed tighter to the metal staircase leading down to the deck and made sure Ana was okay. Maddie didn't miss the look of determination on the young girl's face, but she also knew that Ana needed to be resting somewhere safe…not on the deck of a sinking boat.

"Maddie?" Grant called down to her from above.

"We're okay."

For now. Maddie looked out at the sea of passengers camped on the deck. Something was going to have to change quickly.

She watched as an orange meteor-like object flew out of a flare in an arch above them. The crew was already at work on the lower deck, handing out life jackets to passengers.

Maddie pulled one of the crew members aside, shouting above the noise of the passengers. "I'm a doctor. If there's anything I can do to help—"

"One of the other crew hit his head a few minutes ago."

Grant nodded at her. "I'll watch Ana. Go."

The story from the Bible of the little boy and the five loaves of bread and two fishes popped into her mind, as she hurried after the crew member. *Lord, we could sure use a miracle.*

In facing death daily, she'd learned the simple truth

that no one was promised another day. Life could be snuffed away in the blink of an eye. Because of that, she'd tended to look at each day as a gift. Keeping that in mind once more, she pushed away her negative thoughts and focused instead on the situation before her. She needed to do what she could to help anyone who was injured.

Out of the corners of her eyes she caught Alistair busy recording the confusion with his camera. But her focus went immediately to the man lying on the ground, eyes opened but with a bump already beginning to form on his head.

Maddie ignored what was going on around her and squatted down beside the man. "My name's Maddie Gilbert and I'm a doctor. I understand you hit your head," she said in Portuguese.

He nodded.

"Can you tell me your name?"

He blinked a couple times. "Bento."

"Okay, Bento. Do you know what day it is?"

"Monday."

"Good. I need you to do something else for me." She placed her finger about twelve inches from his face. "I want you to follow my finger with your eyes. Can you do that?"

She watched his reaction while she moved her finger side to side, then up and down. "You're going to be fine, Bento. Can you tell me how you got this bump on your forehead?"

He grabbed on to the metal rail beside him and started to pull himself into a sitting position.

"Whoa…be careful," she said. "Are you sure you can sit up?"

He nodded.

"Okay. Nice and steady. Bento, do you remember what happened?"

"I was just walking across the deck. The ship jerked, and I lost my balance. Hit my head on this railing."

"I've just got a couple more questions, then," she said. They were lining everyone up around them, ensuring they had life jackets. She ran through the list of possible symptoms of a concussion with him.

"No, just a headache where I smacked it."

Maddie grabbed a flashlight from her bag. "I'd like to do one last thing, Bento. I'd like to check your eyes with my flashlight, is that okay?"

Bento nodded.

Maddie watched the pupils constrict as they focused on the light. "I think you're okay, but if you start having any strange symptoms, like vomiting, headaches, problems with balance or light, I want you to find me, okay?"

Someone shouted behind them. In all the confusion, it took a moment for Maddie to realize there was a man running toward her with a child in his arms. Blood ran down the young boy's face.

"I heard you were a doctor." The man's eyes pleaded with her. "Please…you must help my son."

TWELVE

The wind tugged at Maddie's hair as the man pleaded with her for help. She pushed the loose strands back from her face. Grant had come here to rescue her. To protect her. How had it managed to come to this downward spiral of events? Sam's murder... Reid Johnson wanting her dead... A sinking ferry quickly turning into an ER...

She felt the restless crowd press in around them.

"Grant, I'm going to need your help. We need to get the boy upstairs on one of the benches. It's too crowded for me to take care of this here on the deck."

She gave the father instructions in Portuguese and reached for her bag.

Antonio grabbed Ana's hand. "I'll stay with her down here."

Maddie nodded her thanks and motioned for the father to take the boy up the metal stairs, while Grant followed behind them. Inside, the television still droned on in the background, but beside that, all that was left in the VIP room was a trail of food wrappers and a couple water bottles people had left behind in the panic to get to the deck.

"Tell me what I can do," Grant said.

"I need a pair of latex gloves and a couple of the compress dressings." She helped the father situate the boy on one of the benches. "We need to get him cleaned up first so I can see just how bad this cut is."

Grant unzipped her bag, while she tried to calm the boy, who couldn't be more than six or seven.

"You took quite a tumble, didn't you?" she said, catching the fear in his eyes.

A big tear slid down his face as he nodded, clearly trying to be brave.

"What's your name?"

"Marco."

"Marco, I'm going to have to clean this cut up, okay? And I know it looks like a lot of blood, but it doesn't look like it's really that bad," Maddie said, pulling on the latex gloves Grant had handed her. She took one of the water bottles and carefully began to wash the four-inch gash just above the boy's temple.

"Can you tell me what happened?" she asked the father.

"He fell when the boat jolted and his head struck a piece of sharp metal. There's so much blood. My wife… I'm meeting her in Bissau…if anything happens to our son…"

"Your son is going to be fine. When someone has a cut on their head, it tends to bleed a lot. I'm going to finish cleaning this up and then I'll decide whether or not he needs stitches. I just need you to help keep him calm."

A minute passed as she cleaned the wound and asked him some routine medical questions. "It's deep enough for him to need stitches. There's a packaged suturing kit in one of the front pockets," she said while jutting out her chin toward the backpack.

Grant pulled out the single-use suturing tray. "This is impressive. Needle, scissors, gauze…"

"At least I can take care of this situation." She laid out the supplies next to the boy on the poly-lined drape that had come with the kit. It wasn't as if she'd packed her bag that day intending to treat a cholera epidemic. Or discover someone wanted her dead. "I need you to hold the flashlight above the wound, so I can stitch it up."

Standing beside her, Grant aimed the light directly on the injury.

"I used to think conditions at the hospital up north of the country in Bolama were primitive," she said to Grant in English, as she began to sew up the wound. "I never imagined I'd be doing a medical procedure on a ferry taking on water in the middle of the ocean."

Grant laughed. "Not exactly a scenario I'd ever dream up, either."

"You're not squeamish, are you?" Looking up briefly, she threw Grant a grin before making another stitch. "I had a student nurse pass out on me last week when I went to sew someone up."

"I hate snakes, remember, not needles."

She laughed. "I'll buy that. You are a former marine and work as a deminer. Not exactly professions for the squeamish. But you want to hear a secret of mine?"

"Of course."

"I've always hated needles."

"You hate needles…you're kidding."

"It was the one thing I almost let get between me and medical school."

"And now?"

"Thankfully I learned that watching injections or suturing, and being the one doing it, are different. As long as I'm holding the needle, I'm fine."

She worked to finish suturing the wound, wondering why she felt an urge to open up to him. Wondering if the rapid heartbeat didn't have more to do with the man standing next to her than the situation they were in. And her dislike of needles wasn't the only confession she wanted to make. She wanted to tell him how much she enjoyed being around him, how she wanted time to get to know him better, and that him just being here had given her the courage she knew she was going to need to ensure Reid Johnson ended up being accountable for what he'd done.

"Finished." Ignoring her heart, Maddie clipped the thread with a pair of scissors and carefully bandaged the wound.

"Are you sure he's going to be all right?" the father asked.

"Might leave a little scar, but he's as good as new." She grinned at Marco. "And you have been very, very brave."

Grant pulled a peppermint candy from his pocket and handed it to Marco, who rewarded Grant with a smile.

She gave the boy's father instructions in Portuguese on how to care for the wound and watched as he carried the young boy away. Hopefully, this injury would be the worst thing that happened to this little boy tonight.

Grant helped her clean up in silence and then turned to her. "Before someone arrives with another emergency, do you have time for me to show you something?"

"As long as this ship doesn't sink," she said, putting away the rest of her supplies. "Because actually I've got all the time in the world. We're not exactly going anywhere."

"Good, because I didn't notice this before, but there's a small balcony attached to this room on the back of the ferry."

She stepped out in front of him onto the small ledge that was surrounded by a rusty iron railing. The heavy early-morning mist and storm clouds had begun to dissipate, leaving behind a clear azure-blue sky with barely a whisper of cloud to obscure its intense color.

She leaned against the railing and let the wind blow against her face. "Wow. From here, I can almost forget what's going on around us. It's beautiful, isn't it?"

"I thought you could use a short reprieve."

She looked at him and felt her stomach dip, but she wasn't sure she could tell the conflicting emotions apart anymore. Worry over what might happen mingled with anticipation. And even though the magnetic pull she felt toward him seemed dwarfed by her own fear, she couldn't deny the way he affected her. And it went beyond the spicy scent of his cologne and his nearness at the moment.

Which was also making it very difficult to shove aside the resolutions she'd made when it came to guarding her heart. After Ben, she'd convinced herself she didn't want a rebound relationship. That she wanted a chance to focus on her humanitarian work. And that she was perfectly content being single.

Which she had been. Until Grant had waltzed back into her life.

Somehow he'd begun to make her wonder if all of her excuses were simply that. Excuses.

"You okay?" he asked.

"It's been a challenging day," she said finally. "Okay...a challenging week. Do you really think this ferry could sink?"

"I'm not sure, but at least we're still afloat, which is good news."

"Right. She leaned back against the rail, liking his optimism. Liking the way he had a habit of going against the odds. And winning.

She tried to ignore the murmur of voices from the deck below and tried to concentrate on what was okay.

The warm sun that was finally out. The fact that they *were* still afloat. That Reid Johnson had no idea where they were. And that Grant was here with her.

"What I do know," he continued, "is that I'm impressed with the way you handle things. Even with your medical preparation, today hasn't been easy. You have this knack of taking the knowledge you were trained with and making do with the few resources you have."

"I've only done what's needed." She turned back toward the sea, trying to brush away the compliment.

"Maybe, but you've managed to step outside your comfort zone, one where you have almost unlimited resources, to a place where doctors are in short supply and diseases are rampant, and make it work. It's been...it's been a long time since I met someone who possessed the inner strength you have."

She stared out across the sea, knowing she was blushing. "I'm not the only one. You can't tell me you do your job just for the money."

"No, but I'm not always sure my reasons are very noble, either."

She took a chance and searched his expression, wondering if guilt from losing Darren played a part.

A drop of rain hit the tip of her nose, and he leaned forward to brush it off.

She couldn't move. He was close enough she could feel his breath on her face. Close enough he could almost make her forget everything that was going on around them. And he definitely made her want to kiss him. She turned away from him finally, so he couldn't read her expression, and let her gaze settle back on the gray-blue waters beyond them. Because one kiss and she knew she'd never be the same again.

Grant wanted to ignore the unexpected moment that had just passed between them. Because what if he'd misread her? Or misinterpreted her body language. But he'd seen something in her eyes as she'd looked up at him, and knew he couldn't just walk away this time.

Settling down with a good woman is a good thing. And worth it. It's time you got married and had a couple kids. It will quickly show you what's important in life. Things like family.

Antonio's words replayed in the back of his mind. Running was easy. He knew how to do that. Putting himself in a position of vulnerability was hard. He'd been using his job as a sort of wall he'd erected around himself. The one guarantee that he'd keep his distance and protect his heart.

Somehow, though, Maddie had continued to chip her way through the weak spots of those walls.

The boat jolted again beneath them. He pulled her

against him and steadied them both. He had to find a way to keep her safe. Not just from their current situation, but from Reid as well.

"It sounds like they're trying to get the engines working," he said, "but we still don't seem to be moving."

She rested her hands against his chest, making no attempts to pull away from him. "What if we don't manage to make it off this boat alive? What would be your one regret?"

"That I missed the chance to get to know you better." He spoke before he had a chance to think through his response. But Antonio had been right. She was the one thing that made sense in this situation.

A smile played on her lips, melting through another corner of his heart. "That would be your one regret?"

He hesitated, knowing it was probably foolish to even go there right now.

He took a step backward, needing to put some space between them. "I don't want you to get the impression that I'm the kind of guy who falls for every pretty girl I meet, but I did have a crush on you back then. And if I'm honest, not much has changed."

The blush was back in her checks. And he was being far too forward.

"I'm sorry," he said.

She shook her head. "No... I admit I had a bit of a crush on you as well."

"Really?" He hadn't expected that.

"But you were always hanging out with Darren and my dad. Talking cars, and football and politics... I never thought you noticed me."

He smiled. "Trust me, I did."

"But then our lives went different ways."

"What about now?" He was stepping on rocky territory. Just because she'd felt something back then didn't mean those feelings were still there. A lot of time passed. She was a different person and so was he.

"What do you mean?" she asked.

"Our lives have managed to overlap again. Completely unexpected."

Am I off on this, God? Am I trying to force something simply because of the crazy situation we're in?

"You did sweep in like a knight in shining armor," she said, "but once this is all over—if this is all over—I don't know. These past few days have been a bit surreal for me. I was convinced I was going to die and then you showed up, and now you've been there each time I needed someone to lean on." Maddie looked up at him, her brown eyes wide with question. "But the truth is, we live in two different worlds. So yes, I do feel something. I just don't know how things could ever work between us."

"Maybe it is just the intensity of what's happened, but I think you're wrong." Grant struggled for what to say. He'd been certain the interest he felt wasn't one-sided. And now that he knew he was right, he wasn't ready to simply drop the subject. "We both care about the world around us and are trying to make a difference in people's lives. Why can't we take a chance and see what would happen? No commitments or promises. Just time to get to know each other and see what's there?"

Maddie leaned back against the railing. "We don't even live in the same city, and what happens when they relocate you to another mine-infested country?"

"Email, phone calls." He reached out and let his fingers briefly stroke her arm. "There are always ways to make things work."

"I don't know, Grant." Maddie reached down and played with the hem of her shirt, rolling the fabric between her fingers. "You're a deminer, and to be perfectly honest with you, I don't know if I could live with that."

Her words were like a punch in the gut. "I'm good at what I do, Maddie. Yes, there are dangers, but you can't say your line of work is hazard-free."

"My parents would agree with that assessment." A grin played on her lips as her gaze rose to meet his. "I don't think they'll ever understand why I didn't choose to play doctor in some nice, quiet town. But still, it's not the same. You can't even begin to compare the dangers of what we do for a living."

"Why not?"

"Why not? Because…because you can't."

"What if I can prove it to you?"

"Prove what to me?"

"The fact that we're more alike than different," he said. "Face it, neither of us would be happy working a nine-to-five job and coming home to our nice white picket fence in the suburbs. We both need something more."

"Okay, so we have a thing or two in common. But I'm not that same girl you had a crush on, and I have a feeling you're not the same man you were back then, either."

"True, but I know enough to see that you have a heart for others, and you're not willing to just go with the status quo. You're willing to step out of your comfort zone—"

"That's not enough to base a relationship on."

"No, but it's enough to start a relationship on."

Maddie shook her head. "Even if we do get off this dilapidated cargo boat alive, there are still too many complications. There's also Ben. I might be over him, but I'm not looking for a rebound relationship. And I'm going to be a lot more cautious the next time around."

"Why did you break things off with Ben, anyway?"

Maddie hesitated at his question. It was personal, but the entire conversation had been personal. If she were honest with herself, Grant was everything Ben wasn't. And everything she'd been looking for. Which on one level terrified her. Ben had thrived on structure. He rarely changed his familiar routine. And she'd never completely fit into his world. He'd called her a free spirit. Not to criticize her, but because it had been true. He'd told her she brought balance to his life. But while it might be true that opposites attract, in the end he'd only managed to smother her. Just like her parents had with their plans for her life. And as much as she'd loved all of them, she'd needed the chance to test herself and find out who she really was, both as a doctor and as a woman.

Moving to Guinea-Bissau had given her exactly that.

But the situation she'd been thrown into the past week had also managed to push her toward the edge. Adding Grant to that scenario could only end in disaster.

"I'm sorry," he said, "I never should have pushed. I had no right to—"

"No, it's not that. I don't feel…"

Didn't feel what? Attraction? The desire to give a relationship a chance?

She tugged on the straps of her life jacket, a reminder of what was going on around them, and struggled for what to say. Struggled over the fact that a week ago life as she knew it had somehow changed forever, and now not only was someone trying to kill her, but she was falling for the man who'd swept in to save her.

She was falling for him?

The thought took her by surprise, but she knew it was true. A relationship between them wouldn't work... couldn't work. But somehow, all her excuses didn't seem to matter at the moment.

Why can't we take a chance and see what would happen? No commitments or promises. Just time to get to know each other and see what's there?

What if he was right?

Grant took her hands, and brought them slowly toward his chest. "All I'm looking for is a chance to get to know each other. No strings attached, I promise."

Maddie closed her eyes and breathed in the salty sea air, and knew that as wild as it seemed, that was what she wanted. "Okay."

"Okay?"

She opened her eyes and nodded, wondering if she'd be able to find a way to deal with the fact that he worked as a deminer. And how could she spend every day worrying if he'd come home? Was she really willing to step out on a limb and trust him with her heart? There were so many questions—and the answers seemed as difficult to reach as the land they were seeking. But maybe this—maybe he—was worth taking a chance.

"Maddie…" His voice was tinged with a deep urgency.

Grant's lips met her own with a passion that she hadn't expected. For a moment, the desperate scene around them melted away. Maddie was aware only of the man who held her in his arms and of the growing feelings toward him she could no longer deny.

Shouts resonated from the deck below. She turned around and grabbed on to the railing. "Grant…"

The water level had risen significantly over the past few minutes and now covered a section of the port bow.

"Looks like they're not able to pump out the water as quickly as it's coming in," Grant said. "And the extra weight of the water is destabilizing the vessel."

He didn't have to say anything else. Beyond a certain point—if too much water was taken on—the ferry would capsize. There weren't enough lifeboats for all the passengers and only a handful of buoyed rings.

"Do you really believe we're going to sink?" she asked.

Grant squeezed her hand. "I don't think it's a question any longer of *if*, but of *when*."

THIRTEEN

Panic was settling over the deck as Grant hurried behind Maddie down the metal steps. They needed to get to the other side, where the ferry was still out of the water, but cargo was shifting on the deck as waves crashed over the sides, making their progress difficult.

How had it come to this?

Reid Johnson had managed to set off a chain of events with Maddie's abduction that had spiraled their situation completely out of control.

Grant paused at the bottom of the stairs, searching for the best route across the deck while some of the crew attempted to move cargo from the port to the starboard side. Antonio and Ana were somewhere where the crew was gathering the passengers. If this ferry sank now, the loss of life was going to be heavy.

"What do you think they're doing?" Maddie shouted above the chaos.

Crewmen shouted orders, and babies cried, while goats and chickens were making a ruckus where they were tied up.

"Looks like they're moving cargo and gear to the opposite side of the leak in hopes of tilting the leak above the waterline."

"Do you think that will work?"

"I don't know, Maddie." He grabbed her hand. "But we need to get to the other side of the ferry."

Because what he did know was that water was coming in fast. Antonio had mentioned they might have hit a sandbar. If that was the case, there was a chance it would keep their position fixed above the waterline until help arrived. Which might end up being their only way to avoid disaster.

They headed toward the rest of the passengers, still searching for Antonio and Ana. They were here, somewhere, amid a sea of weathered orange life jackets, but so far he hadn't been able to find them. They'd almost made it to the railing when something caught his attention along the horizon.

"Wait a minute, Maddie…" He pulled her toward him and squeezed her hand. "I think the cavalry's just arrived."

Half a dozen fishing boats were making their way toward the ferry.

Thirty minutes later, Grant blew out a sigh of relief as he and Maddie took the last fishing boat. They'd found Antonio and Ana, who were on their way to the island in the boat ahead of them. Behind them, the ferry tilted at a forty-five degree angle, lodged against a sandbar: the only thing keeping a section of the deck above the water. The fishermen had made room for passengers with their boxes of palm wine, petrol cans and livestock. Sails made out of nylon food-aid bags fluttered in the breeze above them. With the afternoon sun sparkling against the blue expanse of ocean around them, he sent up a prayer of thanks. They might not have made it to the capital, but at least they were all alive.

He sat beside Maddie along with a couple dozen

other passengers, trying to avoid stepping in the mixture of fish parts and mud at the bottom of the boat. Palm trees waved in the breeze, seeming to welcome them to the island. He was simply grateful they'd been able to avoid the ferry sinking completely.

Gripping the side of the rocking boat where they sat along the edge, he watched the ferry continue to sway in the distance with each wave that struck. "I don't know about you, but once we get to shore, it's going to be a while before I have any desire to get on another boat."

"You're not the only one," Maddie said following his gaze out across the choppy ocean. "But it could have been a whole lot worse."

Sobering thoughts of what could have happened hovered at the forefront of his mind. But now that the crisis was over, he couldn't help but shift his thoughts back to Maddie. He followed the curve of her lips and wondered what she thought about their unexpected kiss. It wasn't that he regretted his actions. Not at all. She'd managed to completely captivate him. And kissing Maddie had been everything he expected—and more. He did wonder, though, what she thought now that the intensity of the moment was over and their lives were no longer hanging in the balance. He needed to find out.

Staring out at the whitecaps rolling in, he tried to battle the uprising of nerves that had settled in his gut. "Maddie, I've never been one to mince words…"

He paused, still not sure what to say, because at the moment, the very opposite seemed true. Even deactivating a land mine didn't have the overwhelming effect that she had on him. He cleared his throat and tried to start over. "Because I deal with deadly situations every day, I tend to grasp hard at life and what's put in front of me. On one hand, it's made me appreciate more what I have, but on the other hand, my way of 'seizing the moment like a detonating time bomb' has got me in a peck of trouble a time or two. What I'm trying to say is, if I offended you earlier…"

"By kissing me?" A soft blush splashed across Maddie's cheeks.

"Yeah."

And I sure would love to kiss you again right now…

"Don't worry." The corners of her mouth curled into a grin. "If I hadn't wanted you to kiss me, you'd have ended up flat across the deck."

"Ha-ha, ouch! Remind me to be more careful around you." It was this same fire and passion that had drawn him to her in the first place. And the very thing that had him longing for the chance that something could develop between them.

"Yeah…you'd better watch it."

He felt relieved at her playful reaction, because he didn't want there to be any regrets between them. Regrets over the past, or regrets later over what might happen.

A couple of the fishermen jumped out of the boat in thigh-deep water.

He saw Maddie lean back to check the water level. "We're stopping here?"

"Because of the tides we're going to have to wade to shore," one of the fishermen said.

Grant watched a man balance his belongings on his head and start toward land. People started following him, dropping over the side of the boat carrying sacks, chickens and children.

"There is good news," Grant said. "From what I understand, this island has a number of tourist hotels.

Think of a comfortable bed, a hot shower and meals on the veranda. And while it might not be the mainland, we might be able to find us a telephone that works."

Grant slipped into the water behind Maddie. "You okay?"

"I had been hoping to avoid getting wet through all of this, but I'm fine. But I hope those hotels you mentioned are five-star hotels where I can get a three-course meal. And I'm talking line fish, buttery mashed potatoes and chocolate mint tart with ganache like my mother makes."

"I'll certainly see what I can do. I might even be able to throw in an after-dinner show."

She laughed at his attempts at humor. "Actually, all I really want right now is a hot shower."

She slowed down as they waded onto the shore and grasped his arm. "Do you think Reid can find us here?"

"I think he'll assume we're going to the mainland. I heard one of the crewmen say that a cargo boat was on its way here now to transport all the passengers to the mainland."

"And us? What do you think we should do?"

"I think we need to stay here and arrange to catch a ride out tomorrow with Colton at the airstrip. Which should mean no Reid *and* no more boat rides." He ran his thumb down her cheek. "So all you need to worry about now is a hot shower, dinner and a good night's sleep."

Maddie let the lukewarm water wash away the grime that had collected over the past few days. It felt like heaven to be clean again. Breathing in the flowery aroma of the cherry blossom body wash her mom had sent her, she let out a contented sigh. If it were up to her, she'd be perfectly content to stay under the warm water in the tiled bathroom with its mint-green fixtures for the rest of the afternoon.

Instead, she stepped out of the shower onto a thick mat, towel dried and slipped on her purple sundress. The steam fogging the bathroom mirror had gotten rid of most of the wrinkles, but wrinkles or not, compared to what she'd been wearing this past week, a set of clean clothes and shampooed hair felt like heaven.

Gone were the antiseptic smells of the makeshift infirmary in the rebel camp and the constant bleating of goats and squawking of chickens on the ferry. Thanks to the manager of a local hotel, they'd managed to book two of the rooms with breathtaking views of the sea.

Grant's image came to mind as she pulled out the lip gloss her mom had sent her and thought about his kiss—something she'd been unable to forget the past few hours. Maybe it had just been the moment. Tough situations always intensified feelings. What she'd been through the past week had left her feeling vulnerable and exposed, and he'd stopped all of that. Because she knew they would have killed her if Grant and Antonio hadn't shown up to rescue her.

What do I do, Lord? Our lives are heading in separate directions, and when all of this is over...

Would that change everything? She'd planned to move back to the United States by Christmas, but she still had no idea what her next step was going to be. She'd been assured when she left nine months ago that she could step back into her old practice. But she'd also been considering signing up for another nine months right here in Guinea-Bissau.

She stared at her reflection and caught the dark circles under her eyes. The past week had drained her both physically and emotionally. But she also didn't miss the hint of brightness in her face. A gratefulness for being alive, along with an assurance that all of this would be over soon. Definitely. But she knew the way she felt wasn't just due to her relief that they were off that boat. Because as much as she didn't want to admit it, she knew Grant was part of the reason.

Where he fit into the picture, though, she still had no idea.

She pulled out the letter he'd given her from her mother and stepped out onto her room's patio, careful not to wake Ana who'd quickly gone back to sleep after the afternoon's ordeal on the water.

Outside, Maddie sat down beneath a wide umbrella on one of the mocha-colored cushioned lounge chairs that overlooked the sea, still fingering the letter. She held it up and inhaled the subtle scent of her mother's perfume, before opening up and reading it again.

My Dearest Madison,

I have no words to even begin to express what I am feeling at this moment, because I don't know if you're even alive. Fear, dread, panic…none of those words seem adequate. I don't even know if you will see this letter. Or if you'll ever walk through the front door again. And I don't want to go through that again.

When I watched you board that plane earlier this year, I knew that once again I had to let you go and let God take complete control. But I'll be honest. Letting go hasn't been easy, and I've managed to fight Him the entire time. In some ways it was like the first day I sent you off to kindergarten, except this time the stakes are higher. Because I don't know where you are, who has you, or how to get you back.

There are literally hundreds praying for your return right now. Jamie has set up a Facebook page, and I can't keep up with the comments. But I can feel their prayers and God moving, because sometimes that sliver of faith is the only thing I have left. And because we won't stop until you are home.

Which is why, while you read this letter, I'm going to assume that you're with Grant, and he's bringing you home to me. He offered to bring you a small bag of things you might need and, being the practical person I am, I included deodorant and clean underwear. I'm assuming you will greatly appreciate both.

We put up the tree last night so it would be ready for you when you get back. The lights, the stockings on the fireplace, everything is ready for your return. Because I have to believe that Grant will do everything in his power to keep his promise and bring you home for Christmas.

I won't go into how hard this is for me. How I've already lost one child and don't know how to face losing another. So I will simply keep praying that God will answer my prayer this time and that Grant will find a way to bring you back safely.

I will see you soon. I have to believe that.
Mom

Maddie tucked the letter under her leg and leaned back against the cushions. Grant had told her they needed to wait to call her family. Reid would be expecting them to contact her parents. Which meant they had to assume it wasn't safe. While she didn't want to put her life at risk or the lives of her family, she needed them to know she was okay. Needed them to know that she was alive and all this would be over soon.

At least that was what she was praying was going to happen. An end to the fear and panic that still gripped her. She closed her eyes, the afternoon sun warm against her legs, suddenly realizing how sleepy she was.

She was safe. Grant was nearby, and Reid couldn't find her here.

Maddie sat up with a start. Grant's towering figure loomed above her. He'd shaved and changed into a pair of shorts and a chocolate-colored T-shirt he must have had stashed in his backpack. She couldn't stop the buzz of contentment that swept through her.

He sat down across from her on the second lounge chair. "I'm sorry. I didn't mean to scare you."

"No…it's fine. I must have fallen asleep." She sat up, put her feet on the ground beside the chair—their knees almost touching—and took a second to orient herself. Except for a bird chirping in the background, and the waves lapping against the shoreline, it was quiet. And instead of the foul odors of the cargo boat, all she could smell was the spicy scent of Grant's cologne.

He handed her a glass of fresh mango juice.

"Thanks." Maddie took a sip. "Mmm…this is good. What time is it?"

"Just after six. Almost time for dinner. I thought this might wake you up."

"I didn't mean to sleep so long."

"You needed it."

"I guess so." She held up her arms for inspection and ran her fingers across her face. "I'm not burnt, am I?"

"Nope. Except for your toes and these bright red nails, you're still pretty much in the shade." Grant laughed. "Feel better?"

"Yes, actually. Much better. Though I need to check on Ana—"

"She's fine." Grant put up a hand to stop her. "She went for a walk along the beach with Antonio. She's feeling better."

"The manager sent someone to the pharmacy to get me what I needed for her. I'll need to watch her, because it's normal for the symptoms to come and go in cycles, but she should be on the mend."

Both were silent as they watched the dazzling African sun drop into the horizon. The oranges and yellows exploded across the water as the ball of fire made its final descent. Tomorrow they would fly out of here, and in another couple days, as soon as they could get Sam's information into the right hands, she'd be able to go home. Maybe she would actually make it home in time for Christmas.

The wind caught the edge of her mom's letter and blew it across the veranda. Maddie hurried to pick it up before it flew away and frowned. Because while she might make it home for Christmas, right now she knew her family was struggling with not knowing what was going on.

"What's that?" he asked.

She held up the pink stationery with her mother's monogram at the top. "It's the letter you brought me from my mom. They have no idea what's going on. They don't know if I'm dead or alive. And I have to admit, I'm struggling not to simply head back into that hotel lobby and call them."

He waited until she sat back down and then took her hands. "I know it's hard, but you just need to wait a little bit longer. We have to make sure Reid can't find us until we can turn over the evidence we have to the proper authorities. When I can ensure your safety, then we'll call. But this isn't the place."

She knew he was right. Reid had resources, and it was still possible he could track them down here. All they had to do was make it till morning, and they'd finally be out of his reach.

FOURTEEN

Maddie took a bite of the omelet on her breakfast plate the next morning and let out a contented sigh. The storm clouds from yesterday had completely vanished during the night, leaving behind a bright blue sky with only wisps of white clouds hugging the horizon of the sparkling Atlantic. The hot shower and a full night's sleep in a proper bed had done wonders to her frame of mind. Which was why much of the fear that had so tightly encased her over the past few days had slowly started to fade.

But not completely.

Reid had visited her in her dreams. He'd taunted her as she struggled to swim to shore. Large waves had slammed into her as she'd fought the swirling dark waters in order to stay alive.

She couldn't forget he was still out there. Not yet.

"Could you imagine yourself here forty-eight hours ago?" Grant asked.

"No." She forced her mind away from the lingering hold of her nightmares. "It feels like paradise. Especially after all that's happened."

She'd thought she was going to die. And while she

knew it wasn't over yet, in a couple hours Colton would deliver them to a safe house and they'd hopefully have the answers they were looking for.

And even more importantly, she would finally be safe.

She took another bit of her omelet. "Not only is the setting perfect, but I don't believe I've ever eaten a meal that tasted as good as this one."

Grant shot her a smile. "You said that last night at dinner."

"Well, it's true." She laughed and took a sip of her juice. "It's been days since I sat down and ate a decent meal without worrying if it was going to be my last."

The large terrace off the hotel lobby was filled with tables where they sat overlooking the gardens with their stunning pink and orange flowers and a swimming pool. Beyond the pool lay a stretch of white sand and then the sea, which had finally calmed.

Perfect meal.

Perfect view.

She stole a look at Grant. And perfect company.

"You're sure Colton's coming?" she asked. Now was not the time to reassess her feelings toward Grant.

"Yes."

"And Reid has no way to connect the two of you?"

"None." Grant reached out and clasped her hand. "Which is why this is all going to be over soon. I promise."

Antonio stepped out of the lobby and headed toward them across the veranda. The moment he caught her gaze she knew something was wrong.

"Antonio?" Maddie felt the panic returning. "What's wrong?"

"We need to settle our bill and get out of here."

"What's wrong?" Maddie dropped her fork onto her plate.

"There's a television in the hotel lobby," Antonio said. "Our faces have been plastered all over the national news, thanks to yesterday's boat incident."

"What?" Grant stood up. "How?"

"Alistair," Maddie said. A sick feeling flooded through her. "He was taking photos all afternoon."

"And your face is the one they're running the most," Antonio said. "Doctor treats patients as ferry sinks."

"Where is he now?" Grant asked.

"He returned on the other boat last night," Antonio said, "so sometime between his arrival and now, the story was picked up by the local news channel."

"That means if Reid didn't know where we were, he does now." Grant set a couple bills on the table and signaled to their waiter to let him know they were leaving. "You're right. We need to go."

Maddie looked to Grant, wondering if there was going to be anywhere that she was going to feel safe. "Where?"

"They'll probably search the local hotels first," Antonio said, "Which won't take long. When is your pilot friend supposed to be here?"

Grant glanced at his watch. "About an hour and a half. He wanted to avoid flying in the dark."

"Then we need to be at the airstrip waiting for him," Antonio said.

"What if they're watching the airstrip?" Maddie asked.

"We'll have to be careful, but I think it's a chance

we have to take. We need to get off this island. Where's Ana?"

"She went to play with the manager's daughter," Maddie said, standing up.

"Maddie, go grab your and Ana's things," Grant said. "Antonio, if you'll find us a taxi, I'll get Ana."

Movement caught her eye along the shoreline. Maddie froze, but it was nothing more than a pair of flamingos feeding on shrimp. Still, she hadn't missed the fear in Antonio's eyes. She'd been foolish to imagine somehow that they wouldn't be able to find them here. That they'd outsmarted Reid and whoever was working with him.

Because despite her bad dreams, she'd allowed herself to believe there was going to be a happy ending to all of this. Reid would go to prison. Ana would find her grandmother. Grant would get her home by Christmas and the two of them… She pushed back the thought. She couldn't be certain about anything now.

"Maddie?"

She looked up at Grant as Antonio left for the lobby. "If Reid finds us—"

"He's not going to find us."

"You don't know that. Just like before, you can't promise me we're going to get out of this alive."

He grabbed her shoulders gently. "Colton is coming to pick us up. He's got a safe place arranged for us to go to as soon as we land on the mainland. And then we're going to figure out who to go to with the information Sam gave you."

She looked up at him, her eyes wide with question. "What if this corruption runs deeper than simply Reid? We don't know if he's the only one involved in this or if there are others. Sam could have been looking for that information as well."

"I don't have all the answers, Maddie."

"I know. I just feel so...helpless to fix this."

"We both do." He pressed his lips across her forehead, lingering for a few seconds. "Go get your stuff. I'll meet you at your room with Ana."

Inside the room there was little to pack. The few things she'd washed in the sink the night before were already dry. She shoved them into her backpack, took one last look at the empty room and hurried out the door. Grant was arriving with Ana, who was wearing the indigo dress they'd bought her yesterday from the local market. Maddie gave Ana a reassuring smile and nodded at Grant. They could do this. Reid was just one man. There was no way he could get to them this fast. All they had to do was walk through the lobby, out the front door and into the taxi waiting for them.

They headed through the hotel. Past the reception and the TV playing in the background next to a cluster of chairs. Maddie took in a slow breath. Last night before falling asleep, she'd pulled out the Bible her mother had sent her and read about when Elisha and his servant were being chased by the enemy and their city surrounded by horses and chariots. Elisha had told his servant not to be afraid, because God's army was on their side.

There are more on our side than on theirs.

Two uniformed officers walked into the lobby.

One of them stepped forward, his hands behind his back. "Maddie Gilbert and Grant Reese?"

Maddie felt her stomach cinch. Heart pound.

Don't be afraid. There are more on our side than on theirs...

Grant stepped in front of Maddie and Ana. "Can I help you?"

"My name is Eduardo Sambe. I'm with the local police. And while I'm sorry to interrupt your holiday, I need you to come with me."

"Is there a problem?" Grant asked. "We just checked out and were planning on leaving."

"This is a private matter, and I'd prefer not to discuss this here in the middle of the hotel lobby."

"Like I said, we have a car waiting for us. Perhaps another time."

Grant started to step around them, but the man held up his hand.

"Apparently you don't understand. This isn't an invitation to a garden party. This is a police matter. We have a problem."

"What kind of problem?"

"Evidence that you and your friends are involved in trafficking drugs in our country, for starters."

"Trafficking drugs?" The room spun around her. Surely she hadn't heard him correctly. "You can't be serious. What kind of evidence do you have?"

"I am not at liberty to discuss those things. Authorities from the mainland will be arriving on the island shortly. You may discuss any concerns you have with them."

Grant held up his hand in protest. "I'm sorry, but this is a mistake. Maddie Gilbert's story has been all over the international news. She was abducted from your capital and taken to a rebel camp on a nearby island to treat a cholera epidemic. My friend and I came to take her home. She's not involved in trafficking drugs. On the contrary, she's spent the last nine months working in your hospitals."

"I already know who you are, but your guilt or innocence is not for me to decide. I am simply following orders and my orders are to bring you in."

Maddie looked outside where a third officer had stopped Antonio. There had to be someone they could call. Someone who wasn't connected with Reid and who could put a stop to this.

"We need to make a call to our embassy," Maddie said.

"That has already been arranged. A delegate from your embassy in Dakar is on his way here right now. In the meantime, I've been given strict orders to take all of you into custody."

Grant glanced at Maddie before turning back to the officer. "What's the name of the official who's on his way?"

"He's with the US State Department. His name is Reid Johnson."

FIFTEEN

Maddie paced the floor of small office in the back of the local police station that held nothing more than a couple chairs, a desk and an out-of-date calendar on the wall. It was one thing to face being arrested in a foreign country for a crime you'd committed. It was another thing altogether to realize you were facing an arrest because you were being set up. She knew enough to realize that once you left the United States, the laws and penalties of your new host country applied to you. Meaning you left behind any support system, emergency and medical services. The only good thing that had happened today was that they'd allowed Ana to stay at the hotel with the manager and her daughter, which meant she should be safe. For now.

Her gaze rested on a water stain on the wall. What were they supposed to do when the person setting them up was supposed to be the person on their side?

"You're going to wear a hole in the tiles." Grant stopped in front of her and squeezed her hands. "Maddie, look at me. We'll figure a way out of this, just like we have the past few days."

"That officer accused me—us—of trafficking drugs.

This isn't some out-of-towner getting a speeding ticket. We could end up in prison, Grant."

"No," Grant said. "That's not going to happen. He has no proof."

"And you think that's going to stop him?" She sounded hysterical. She could hear it in her own voice. But she didn't care. "You've seen what he's willing to do. Anything it takes to ensure he stays in the clear."

"True, but I also think Reid is terrified he's about to get caught and is planning to cut his losses," Grant added.

"And we're in the way," Antonio said.

Grant pulled her close and started praying out loud. For courage, for wisdom and for deliverance. Maddie wished Grant would never let go. She wanted to feel safe again.

When he was done with his prayer, he tilted up her chin so she had to look at him. "Listen to me, Maddie. Reid doesn't have anything on any of us. *And* he has no proof you know anything, either."

"Does that even matter at this point?"

While Reid might not have real proof, evidence could be planted. Grant and Antonio used as leverage…

"What do you think he's going to do?" she asked.

"He'll probably try to scare you. He wants information. He wants to know what Sam said to you, and who gave Sam that information. Don't admit anything." He brushed back her hair behind her shoulders. "And give me the flash drive."

She wrapped her fingers around the locket. "You don't think it's safe here?"

"Reid's smart. You can't let him find it on your person."

"But we can't lose it. It's the only proof we have."

"Don't worry. I'll find a safe place for it."

Five minutes later, Eduardo came for her, insisting she come alone. Maddie followed him down a narrow hall and, as ordered, stepped into another dingy room that held nothing more than a huge wooden desk, a couple chairs, a file cabinet…and Reid Johnson standing in the center of the room.

For a brief moment reality flooded through her. Reid had really found them. And now what made her chest constrict was the knowledge that he planned to do everything in his power to ensure no one found out his secret. Even if that meant using her as an expendable pawn in his game.

Don't be afraid…

She started praying, wishing she could get rid of the sick feeling niggling in her gut. Wishing she could wake up from the nightmare that had become far too real.

Maddie took in a deep breath. Reid was dressed in khaki pants and a white button-down shirt. Late forties, a few gray hairs along his temple…he was the kind of man who would step into a political dinner with a suit and tie and Colgate smile. And was clearly the kind of man who knew how to play just as dirty. And he was accusing *her* of being involved in drug trafficking?

"Dr. Gilbert. We finally meet in person." Reid Johnson smiled at her as if they were meeting for drinks, not an interrogation at some forgotten third-world police station. "Have a seat, won't you?"

Maddie hesitated but then sat in the empty wooden chair, legs crossed. Arms crossed. "I'd like some answers as to what is going on. The local police are accusing me of being involved in drug trafficking."

He leaned against the edge of the desk. "Are you?"

"Involved in drug trafficking? Are you crazy? Of course not."

"Then I'm sorry you got the wrong impression. No one is accusing you of anything."

He was playing her. She might not be able to see it in his eyes, but she knew this was a game to him.

"Then why are you here?" she asked.

"When an American citizen is abducted abroad, the world watches. When I saw your photo on the news, I thought it prudent to fly here myself and debrief you personally. So please know that I'm here to help."

She dropped her hands into her lap, wanting to believe him. Maybe Sam had made a mistake. Maybe his intel had been off. Surely Reid's position in the government was too high-profile for him to take the kind of risks Sam had accused him of.

"From what I understand," Reid continued, "you were kidnapped and taken to one of the local islands to try to stop a cholera outbreak."

"Yes."

"And that a former marine, along with another man from here, managed to help you escape."

She nodded.

"You're lucky. Columbian and Mexican cartels work closely with local criminal gangs. The men who took you are dangerous. I'm sure your family will be relieved to know you're okay."

Maddie didn't respond, uncertain if he was being sincere, or if his words were laced with a subtle threat. Surely he couldn't touch her family.

"Before I arrange for transportation for you and your friends back to the mainland," he continued, "there is another problem that has been brought to my attention involving a journalist by the name of Sam Parker. I understand you treated him the night he was shot."

Sam Parker.

Maddie clenched her fists. Of course Sam was why Reid was here. Not some heroic attempts to debrief and rescue her. Reid knew about Sam. Knew Sam had talked to her. She'd been right all along. Reid was simply playing games.

"I didn't know Sam. He was simply brought in with a gunshot wound, and I treated him. Unfortunately, I couldn't save him. He died in my care from massive internal bleeding."

Reid picked up a pencil off the desk and started tapping it beside him. "Was he ever lucid long enough to hold a conversation?"

"He was in and out of consciousness the entire time."

"I need to know what Sam Parker told you before he died." He kept tapping. Slowly. Precise. Rhythmic. "The quicker I can get the answers I'm looking for, the quicker we can all go home. So please, start from the beginning and tell me about your contact with him. Anything he might have said to you."

Maddie held his gaze. This was Reid's game. Authoritative yet charming. In control. But she wasn't going to play along. And he wasn't going to win.

"Sam was shot outside his hotel just over a week ago," she began.

"The Hotel Decembre."

Maddie nodded. "A witness to the shooting brought him in. I was his primary physician and treated him for a gunshot wound to the chest. He died in my care five hours later."

"I understand you'd been working up north in one of the more rural hospitals. In one of the woman's maternity wards, which is more your specialty."

"I was. But we routinely shift hospitals depending on the need. I was spending two weeks in Bissau, doing some extra teaching rounds."

"Back to that night. Did Sam say anything to you that night?"

"He was in a lot of pain. I was working to save his life. So like I said, there wasn't exactly a lot of time for conversation."

"But he did talk to you, didn't he?"

"Why all the questions about Mr. Parker?"

"Before he died, he was being investigated for his involvement in this country's drug trafficking."

Maddie fought to keep her voice level. Calm. "I heard he was a journalist."

"He was. On paper, anyway. Do you know how much money is involved in trafficking? It's a pretty lucrative business."

"I wouldn't know."

"Are you sure, Doctor?"

"Of course I'm sure."

"Because when I investigated Mr. Parker's involvement in the drug trade, your name came up as well."

Maddie swallowed hard. The fear was back again. But that was what he wanted. "Your source is wrong."

He smiled. "My source says that you frequently offered individuals jobs as drug mules in exchange for family members to receive the treatment they needed. What is a family supposed to do when a child needs a shunt put in…or a burn victim needs treatment…or a preemie needs special care?"

Maddie stood up, her fear quickly morphing into anger. "You've got to be kidding me."

"Sit down, please." Any trace of a smile was gone. "At least fifty tons of cocaine go through this area every year. That is around two billion dollars shipped by drug mules on commercial flights."

"You can't seriously think I'm involved."

"They are always looking for easy targets. Women who are not only inexperienced but financially vulnerable, who need money to support their families and who will agree to act as mules. You have access to families in need of medical care—"

"I'm a doctor here on humanitarian mission, working in the local hospitals. I would never withhold treatment to coerce someone to work as a mule."

Maddie stopped and sat back down. Fighting wasn't going to work. It was all a lie and he knew it. Grant had been right. He wanted to scare her.

"Granted, you don't fit the typical stereotype. But you're also the kind of person no one would suspect."

"Like I said, your source is wrong." Maddie rubbed the back of her neck with her fingertips, wondering what kind of nightmare she'd just stepped into. She knew on one level that what Reid said was accurate. She'd read about what was going on. There were people who made the risky trip to Europe for the money it brought them. A dangerous albeit tempting way out of poverty. They either swallowed cocaine packets or hid them in their luggage, all for a few hundred dollars paid out with a successful handover.

"Let's stop playing games, shall we?" He was tapping again. "I know Sam talked to you. I want whatever information he gave you, along with his source."

"The man was dying, which is why I'm pretty sure he wasn't thinking about his job." Maddie kept her voice steady. "He never gave me any information."

Reid snapped the pencil in two. "Maybe I'm not communicating this to you well enough. Do you know the punishment for trafficking drugs?"

"You're threatening me?"

"It's just a simple question."

"I have no idea."

"In Europe the average is five to twenty years. There are also some countries that allow for the death penalty for drug importation. It depends on what you're carrying, or if you're a courier or have a leading role."

"Then why would I take such a foolish risk?" she asked.

"Don't sound so noble. Money can buy anything."

"Including your loyalty and integrity? Not everyone. Not me."

"Everyone has a price, Doctor." He dropped the broken pencil onto the desk. "You're saying you've never been tempted."

"Tempted? Yes. To betray everything I believe in for a handful of drug money? Never."

He grabbed her backpack, unzipped it and dumped the contents across the table.

"What are you doing? These are my medical supplies and—"

"Where is it?"

"What?"

"Sam had a flash drive. I need that flash drive."

Maddie could feel her heart pounding in her throat. *I don't know what to do, God... This man will do anything to cover his tracks...*

"I've already told you. I was Sam's doctor. That was all. You can look in that bag, and I promise you won't find anything other than medical supplies."

He rummaged through the contents, then dumped out a bottle of pills and threw the container across the room. "And I told you to stop playing games. Tell me where Sam got his information."

"I don't know."

"Really? Because I spoke to a man early this morning. His name's Alistair Hunter. Does that ring a bell?" Reid didn't wait for her to respond. "He knew nothing about your abduction story, but he was thrilled that his photos had helped locate you. And he told me something else. He said you borrowed his computer because you needed to read a flash drive."

Maddie felt her heart plummet. There was no use pretending.

"Maybe Sam didn't tell you the source of his information, but I know he gave you that flash drive, and that you know what's on it. Which makes you a loose end. So here's what's going to happen. You and your friends need to—how do I say it—disappear."

"There are others out there looking for us. You can't just make us disappear."

"That's where you're wrong. You see, there is no law here. Not the way you're used to things working, anyway. Which means you can disappear, and I can blame it on an unfortunate accident. It happens all the time, like the ferry yesterday. This time your plane will go down in the Atlantic, and unfortunately for you, everyone on board will be killed."

"You can't do that."

"Why not?" He took a step toward her and paused. "That's a beautiful locket you're wearing. Was it a gift?"

Maddie swallowed hard and managed to keep his gaze. "Yes, actually. It was."

He yanked it off her neck and popped the locket open. "No photos?"

"No. No photos." Maddie held her breath.

"That's a pity."

He looked up at her again, and smiled, making it clear from his arrogant expression he planned to make good on every one of his threats.

SIXTEEN

Grant glanced at his watch. Trying not to worry had become impossible. Maddie had been in there too long. On top of that, Colton would be arriving in the next thirty minutes, and he had no way of letting his friend know that they once again weren't going to make it to the rendezvous site.

Which meant their odds of escaping this island anytime soon had just dropped substantially, and Reid now knew where to find them.

I'm not sure how, God, but we really need You to step in and fix this mess.

Grant glanced across the room at Antonio, who was leaning back against the wall in one of the wooden chairs on two of its legs, his eyes shut. "How can you sleep right now?"

Antonio opened his eyes, but didn't move. "Someone once taught me the importance of managing my emotions in a crisis. And how remaining calm under pressure was essential to performance. Like when deactivating a land mine, for example."

"Funny." Grant frowned. "This is different."

"Different how?" Antonio let the chair fall forward. "Because Maddie's involved?"

Grant pointed to the door where Sam had placed an armed guard on the other side. "She's out there—more than likely with Reid—a man who was probably involved not only in her abduction, but also at least two other deaths."

"I was right," Antonio said. "You're falling for her. And while I'm not sure why, I think she likes you, too."

Grant pressed his hands against the wall and stared doing a round of pushups. Anything to keep him occupied. "You've always been too perceptive. And far too nosy for your own good."

"But I am right, aren't I?"

"Maybe. And if we make it out of here I might even get the chance to find out."

"*When* we make it. Not if we make it. Reid doesn't have anything on her, or either of us, for that matter."

"You know even better than I do that doesn't matter. Not when you're dealing with corrupt officials. They make the rules." He finished two dozen pushups, took a step back and then shook out his arms. "She's been gone for twenty minutes."

"There is nothing you can do right now."

"There's nothing I can do about a lot of things right now."

"Like with Maddie?"

"I have this gut feeling that in the end she's not going to want a relationship with someone who puts himself in danger so often. And I don't blame her. Because let's face it. Relationships don't always work out like they did for you and Catia."

"Not always," Antonio said. "And maybe you're right. Maybe she's not the one for you, but I've learned that sometimes you have to fight for a happy ending. It wasn't always easy for Catia and I. Her family had expectations. My family had expectations…"

"What made it work?"

"I guess a combination of our stubbornness and our faith. I was lucky to have a couple good examples while I was in the university of relationships that showed me what I wanted."

Antonio had reminded him family was worth the time and the risk. And if Grant was honest with himself, it was what he wanted as well. Because Maddie was the first person in a long time who he could actually imagine building something with. He knew relationships were tough. He knew you had to fight for them. And while he might not have had the examples Antonio had, he knew he wanted something different than his own parents.

Antonio caught his gaze. "I know I'm going out on a limb here, but if you really care about Maddie and think there's a future for the two of you, it might be time for you to move on with your life—even if it means leaving the demining program. One day, you're going to have to face the fact that you're still here because you're still trying to atone for Darren's death."

A seed of anger sprouted. Grant started another set of pushups, wanting to ignore his friend's pointed advice. "This isn't about Darren."

"Isn't it? I might not have been there the day he died, but I do know that sometimes, no matter how hard you try, there's simply nothing you can do to change a situation. And you're never going to be able to go back and change that moment."

Grant had discovered the hard way what horrible twists life could throw at you. Seven months in Somalia had changed them both. But then Grant had returned home alive. And Darren had returned in a coffin.

"It should have been me who died that day."

Grant took a step back from the wall and stopped, surprised by his own words. He'd never admitted to anyone, not even Maddie's parents when he shared what happened the day Darren died, how deep his guilt ran.

"Why?"

He turned around slowly to face Antonio. "If I hadn't pushed him to choose the Marines over his high school girlfriend, Darren would probably be alive right now, happily married with a bunch of kids."

"You don't know that. And it was his choice. Not yours."

His eyes darkened. "Maybe, but I watched him die. And at that moment, I promised myself I would find a way to make up for his death. I finished up my time with the Marines and used my experience to do what I do now."

"Setting out to cleanse yourself from the guilt for being the one who wasn't hurt."

After all the years they'd spent working together, Antonio knew him too well. He didn't know how to walk away from the hold the past had on him. And maybe Antonio was right. In order for there to be any chance of a relationship between he and Maddie—or anyone, for that matter—he was going to have to find a way to let go of the past. And somehow accept the fact that, for whatever reason, God had saved him and allowed Darren to die.

The door opened and Maddie slipped into the room.

"Maddie?" Grant walked across the room, trying to read her expression. "Are you okay?"

She stopped in front of him and rubbed her temples. "Reid accused me of using my position to secure drug mules."

"You've got to be kidding," Grant said.

"He's planning to make us disappear and make it look like an accident."

"What did you tell him?"

"Nothing," she said, "but that doesn't matter. He knows from Alistair that we accessed a flash drive. What he still doesn't have is the person who gave it to Sam."

"So either way, we're still loose ends," Grant said.

"We need a way out of this building," Antonio said. "Is there a guard still outside our door?"

Maddie nodded. "But except for a secretary out front, the place is pretty quiet."

"And Reid? Where's he?"

"I heard him tell Sambe he needed to go make a phone call. I think he might have left."

Antonio stood up and folded his arms across his chest. "Reid might have connections on this island, but so do I."

"What do you mean?" Grant asked.

"That taxi driver I had come pick us up at the hotel is actually an old friend of mine," Antonio said. "He's already picked up Ana and is waiting a couple blocks away to take us to the landing strip. But we only get one shot at this."

"Then it's a chance we have to take," Grant said.

Maddie dropped her hands to her sides. "Is Colton still planning to fly us to Dakar?"

"He's got connections there—"

"So does Reid," she countered.

Grant grabbed her fingertips and squeezed them gently. "We're not going to let Reid win."

"How?" she asked.

"How much time do you think we have till they come get us?"

"I don't know, but I can't imagine Reid wanting to draw this out."

Grant glanced at her backpack, his mind running through their limited options. They had no way to communicate with the outside world, no weapons and they needed a way out. Their only real supplies lay with her medical kit that contained painkillers, gauze, burn creams, cold packs...

Cold packs.

He smiled. "Do you have one of those instant cold packs with your medical stuff?"

"Reid dumped out my stuff searching for the flash drive, but yes... I've still got one."

"Good. Let me have that and a pair of your latex gloves."

"Gloves?" Maddie set down her backpack on the desk and unzipped it. "What are you planning to do? Build a bomb?"

"He's the explosive expert," Antonio said.

"Not a bomb per se," Grant said, taking the cold pack from her. "But if we're going to get out of here, we're going to need a distraction."

Maddie watched while Grant and Antonio worked in silence. Her adrenaline pumped, heart pounding as she wondered if this crazy plan of theirs was actually going to work. Grant might know what he was doing, but time was not on their side. Reid would be back any minute. And when he came back, it was going to be over for all of them.

"Explain what you're doing?" she asked.

"It's basic chemistry. Cold packs are made with ammonium nitrate," Grant began. "And while they're not extremely toxic, when prepared properly, they can produce thick plumes of white smoke."

"You're making a smoke bomb." Apparently she'd slept through that part of Chemistry 101.

"Exactly," he said, working quickly. "I grew up making these things. Guess it was inevitable I ended up working with explosives one day."

Folded sheets of newspaper that had been dipped into the ammonium nitrate solution now lay drying in a patch of morning sunlight on the floor.

"I've got some matches in my backpack," Grant instructed her. "They're in a small, waterproof container in one of the side pockets."

"Okay..." She pulled out the matches and handed them to him. "What else?"

"We need some string." Grant said as he rolled up one of the sheets of newspaper. "Anything that I can wrap around this to hold it together."

Maddie thought quickly. "I've got a roll of gauze."

"Perfect."

Two minutes later they were ready. Grant flung open the door and threw five lit smoke bombs into the narrow hallway in both directions. Through the thick smoke, they hurried out the side door of the small police station.

It might be the distraction they needed, but even in the surrounding chaos, Maddie didn't miss the fact that they were running—again. And she wasn't completely convinced this was going to be enough to get them out of here without getting caught.

She could hear at least one officer was on their tail. She followed Grant and Antonio onto the narrow dirt road, wondering how they were going to make it to the plane. And when she was ever going to feel safe again.

I know You're out there, God. And I know I shouldn't be afraid, but I am.

Because the only way for them to stay alive was to get off this island.

A weapon fired as they skirted around the side of the run-down building following Antonio's lead.

"They're still behind us," Antonio said.

Grant quickly lit the last of the smoke bombs and tossed them toward their pursuers. Maddie's lungs fought for air, both from the smoke and the excursion. They should have stayed. Corruption or not, surely there was no way Reid could get away with his plan. They could have found someone to help them. Someone who would help them stop Reid. Now they'd escaped police custody, the authorities had something valid to pin on them.

But who could they go to? They didn't even know everyone who was involved.

They have money, rifles, ammunition and know every inch of this country's remote areas. They can literally buy the government and do what they want.

Antonio's assessment had been spot-on. The cartel's pockets ran deep, and she wasn't foolish enough to believe Reid was the only one enjoying the benefits.

"We're almost there," Antonio said.

She couldn't hear anyone following them, but that

didn't mean they weren't still there, or that Reid couldn't still find a way to stop them.

She glanced at Grant and a new wave of panic hit full force. Blood seeped through his T-shirt across his shoulder.

"Grant... You've been shot."

"It doesn't matter. We've got to keep moving."

But it did matter. She felt as if she'd just gotten socked in the stomach and couldn't breathe. The past few days had been like a row of dominoes falling in rapid succession, pushing them on toward that ultimate dark moment she knew was coming.

And now she just wanted out.

She could see the car up ahead, but Grant was slowing down. She wrapped her arm around his waist, with Antonio on the other side. At the car, their driver was opening the doors. She slid into the backseat with Grant so she could assess the situation.

Antonio banged on the dash as soon as the last door had shut. "Get out of here now."

"You okay, Ana?" she asked before giving her full attention to Grant.

Ana nodded, eyes wide with fear as another bullet ricocheted off the back of the car.

Whoever had been behind them wouldn't be able to follow them on foot, but she also knew it wouldn't be hard to track them down. There were only two ways off this island. By boat and by air, and Reid knew that.

"So, you think this gunshot wound is life-threatening, doc?" Grant asked.

"It could be worse," she said. "He could have had better aim."

He chuckled, but she could see the pain in his eyes.

She went through her assessment on autopilot. Airway management, respiratory rate, pulse…

Hollywood loved firepower. Villains could get blown away with a single shot, while main characters easily walked away from a bullet wound like it was simply an inconvenience. But in real life, there was no safe place to be shot. Just because the shoulder didn't contain any vital organs didn't mean there couldn't be serious complications. For starters, the subclavian artery that fed the main artery of the arm was there, along with nerve bundles.

And that wasn't the only problem she was facing.

She'd dealt with a number of gunshot wounds in the ER when she'd been on rounds at the hospital, but this time was different. Because this time it was personal.

And because, even all these years after her silly college-age crush, she still felt as if her heart was about to explode out of her chest when he looked at her.

Grant leaned back against the seat and closed his eyes as the car jolted over another bump in the road. "Those crazy smoke bombs worked."

"Yes, they did, but I need you to stay with me, Grant." She applied direct pressure on the wound to stop the bleeding, but he needed to be in an ER with access to a complete trauma team. "Open your eyes, Grant, and talk to me."

He obeyed and looked up at her, wincing at every bump they went over. "Have I told you how pretty you are?"

She ignored his question, and continued checking his vitals. "How are you feeling?"

"Like I was shot."

She smiled. He clearly still had his sense of humor,

but adrenaline was good at blocking out most of the initial pain. The tough part was going to be when the adrenaline wore off.

"So what's the verdict?" he asked.

"Considering how stubborn you are, I'm pretty sure you're going to make it."

She wasn't ready to tell him the truth. That he was losing too much blood and that she could only improvise so much. She was tired of makeshift clinics, the lack of supplies, and having to make do. What if she couldn't save him?

She pushed back the thought. His eyes were closing again.

"Grant…I need you to stay with me."

He wasn't responding.

"I never should have kissed you," she whispered, not even trying to hold back the tears. "Or fallen in love with you."

Fallen in love with him?

No. Maddie pushed closed the door to her heart, wishing she could escape the confines of the car. And his nearness. She'd been a fool to let her emotions go this far.

"Grant?"

She looked outside the car window. Their driver was racing toward the airstrip, past swampy mangroves, but they were running out of time.

"There's the plane," Antonio said.

"Any sign of Reid or his men?" she asked, studying the terrain, her heart pounding.

Antonio shook his head a moment later. "If they are out there, I don't see them."

Maddie swallowed hard, hoping he was right. Because if they weren't here yet, they were on their way.

Colton was waiting for them on the runway.

"He's been shot," she shouted as Antonio helped her get Grant out of the car. Grant moaned at the movement, but at least he was conscious.

"Get in quickly," Colton said. "I can fly you to a hospital on the mainland."

Maddie thanked him as Antonio and Colton helped Grant onto the plane, praying that they made it to the hospital in time to save him. Praying that the men after them didn't find them.

Grant groaned again as she helped him settle into a seat.

"Grant…there's no way you're leaving me now." She said as the plane headed down the remote runway, with still no sign of Reid or his men. "I need you to hang in there."

Please, God…

Because what was happening right now was the very reason she'd hesitated to consider a relationship with him in the first place. Her fear that something would happen to him and she'd end up losing both him…and her heart.

SEVENTEEN

Maddie leaned against the windowsill and watched Grant sleep. The remote missionary hospital, a couple hundred miles from the cluster of islands they'd escaped from, had become a place of refuge for the injured in the province. The long line that waited for medical help outside was proof of that.

It was also where Grant's life had been saved, and—she prayed—where Reid Johnson wouldn't be able to find them. For the moment, there was nothing more she could do but wait and pray that all of this would be over soon. She reached up and rubbed her temples, feeling the tension from her headache slowly spread down her neck and back. After assisting with Grant's surgery, she was exhausted. Dr. Sauer, a surgeon from Alabama who'd performed the operation, had encouraged her to go to the hospital's guesthouse and get some rest, but despite her fatigue she wasn't ready to leave. Not yet.

The doctor had managed to repair the damage left behind by the bullet, which meant, barring an infection or some other unexpected complication, Grant should not only recover completely, but hopefully regain full use of his arm as well.

So why did she still feel so…off course?

The past few hours had been a frightening, but she'd forced herself to lay aside all her emotions and concentrate on Grant simply as a patient, not as someone who'd managed to capture her heart. Now those emotions she'd repressed were threatening to detonate.

An ebony-skinned nurse walked into the quiet room and started taking vital signs of one of the other patients. The long rectangular room, with its pale blue walls, row of beds and a scattering of monitoring machines, was basic, but she'd found the staff to be not only efficient, but compassionate.

"I understand the two of you have been through quite an ordeal." The young nurse smiling across the room at her didn't look like she could be more than twenty.

"It's been a difficult few days," Maddie said. "It's Julia, right?"

She nodded. "I could bring you some tea?"

Maddie smiled at the offer, appreciating her concern. "Thank you, but I'm not going to stay much longer."

"Good, because you look tired. He's going to sleep for a while, but he's going to be fine. You should get some rest. Maybe something to eat."

Maddie knew she was right. She hadn't eaten in hours, and if she didn't get something into her system, she'd be the one needing medical attention. But she wasn't ready to go. Not yet.

"I'm working till midnight," Julia said. "I could give you a call when he wakes up or if anything changes. Are you planning to stay at the guesthouse?"

"Yes, and thank you. I would appreciate that."

Maddie slid into the plastic chair beside Grant's bed as Julia left the room. The pain of almost losing him engulfed her, and not for the first time, she questioned her decision. But in her heart she knew it was what she had to do.

No matter what she felt, there were still certain things she couldn't ignore. Sixty million mines still left unexploded in seventy countries…sixty-five people maimed or killed every day… This was why Grant did what he did. But the facts didn't lie. One of these days, unless he was very lucky, Grant Reese was going to end up another statistic on a humanitarian website. Like her brother. That was something she couldn't face.

The fact was he deactivated land mines for a living.

She'd seen too many maimed bodies. Too many broken spirits. She couldn't deal with that happening again to someone she cared for. Not again.

"I guess I shouldn't be surprised that you're going to make it." She took his hand, careful not to disturb the IV or wake him up. "But you *are* going to make it."

Just not with her.

Grant's face was pale, reminding her of how close they came to losing him. Any longer without the emergency medical care he'd finally received, and he might not have survived. Tears welled up in her eyes, but she wasn't going to cry. She'd cried enough the past few days. Out of frustration. Out of fear. All she wanted to do right now was put all of this behind her.

"How is he?"

Maddie looked up. Antonio stood in the doorway.

"Stable. Resting." She pulled her hand away, and wiped away a stray tear. "The surgery went well. The doctor believes he was able to repair the damage. He'll have to do a few weeks of physical therapy once he's back in the States, but at this point at least, the outlook is good."

"I'm glad to hear that. I'm sorry I haven't been by until now, but I've been working with Colton the past couple hours to figure a way out of our situation with Reid. I'm heading back to the guesthouse now and thought you might want to come with me. Ana's resting there after her doctor's appointment. She's going to be fine."

She smiled her relief. "Thank you for making sure she was okay, so I could stay with Grant during the surgery."

"Of course. I'm just glad he's okay. They're serving dinner soon, and you'll be able to call your parents. With your story already making headlines, I have a feeling Alistair's photos are going to make the news as well. They're going to need to hear what's going on from you first."

She nodded and grabbed her backpack, wondering how much she should tell her mother. Because while the past few hours she'd focused on Grant, she knew that wasn't the only crisis they were facing. As long as Reid was still out there, their lives were still in danger.

"What about Reid?" she asked.

"Colton has been in touch with a contact at the embassy in Dakar."

"Dakar?" She hesitated in the doorway, the fear in her gut pronounced. "Someone we can trust?"

"Yes."

"And?"

"We were able to send him all the contents on the flash drive."

All she could do was pray he was right and that

this was someone who could stop Reid, because they couldn't afford to be wrong. Not on this. But she knew she couldn't keep focusing on the what-ifs. Like what would have happened if Grant hadn't insisted she give him the flash drive? Or if they'd searched Grant before they escaped the police station and found the flash drive. There were simply too many.

Maddie followed Antonio outside the surgical ward, along a brick path that followed the outside wall, faded by the relentless beating of the sun. Women sat with their children, waiting to see a doctor, beneath the overhanging eaves where a slight breeze stirred the late afternoon heat, bringing with it the fragrant scents of the surrounding orange trees that smelled like a mixture of jasmine and honey.

Halfway to the guesthouse that was situated on the far side of the hospital compound, he stopped to face her. "Colton and I found out something else."

"What is it?"

"Reid's secretary was found dead this morning in her home."

Maddie sucked in a breath of air. "She was the one who talked to Sam."

"That's what it looks like. Or at least what Reid thought."

"Then why did he need to question me? Why not just kill us all from the start?"

"Maybe he wanted to make sure he'd sealed off any other leaks. Make sure he wasn't missing someone."

"Where is Reid?"

Antonio started walking again. "They haven't found him yet."

That wasn't the news she'd wanted to hear. "What do you mean they haven't found him?"

"Apparently he left the island not long after we did on his own private plane. But no one knows where he went."

"Do you think he can track us here?"

"It's possible, even though our flight plan was to the capital, not here. We've spoken to the hospital administration. They've agreed to add a few more guards until we leave."

She slowed her steps. Bougainvillea lined the cement wall, purple, white and orange, but all she could see was Reid and his arrogant expression when he'd looked at her. He was going to do anything he could to find her. "There's still a chance we're putting the hospital and everyone at risk here until he's arrested."

"Like I said, we'll take precautions, but I don't think he'll be able to track us here."

She hurried to catch up with Antonio. Maybe he was right, but she'd seen how determined Reid was. He found a way to track them down before. There were no guarantees he wouldn't find a way to do it again.

"How long before it's safe for Grant to travel?" Antonio asked.

"The doctor said he wanted to watch him overnight. I'm sure after that—barring no signs of infection—he'll release him."

"Until then, can I make a suggestion?" he asked as they crossed the lawn in front of the guesthouse.

She nodded.

"Call your parents, eat some dinner and get some rest. Everything will look different tomorrow."

Ten minutes later, she picked up the handset of the

landline and dialed her parents' number. After five rings, she began to wonder if anyone was home. On the sixth ring, the answering machine picked up.

Maddie clicked her fingernails against the top of the desk in the small guest room. She couldn't tell her parents what was going on with a message on the answering machine. But Antonio was right. If they found out through the wrong channels…

The answering machine beeped.

She started to hang up when someone answered.

"Mom?"

"Maddie?

She let out a sigh of relief. "Mom, I'm so glad you're home."

"Where are you? Are you okay?"

She sat down on a padded chair. "It's a long story, but yes… I'm okay."

"When are you coming home?"

Maddie filled in some of the details, saving the rest for when she was with them in person.

"You're sure you're okay?" her mom asked.

"I'm okay. I promise. Because Grant found me, just like he promised. And I'm going to be home for Christmas."

Grant inhaled the bitter odor of the smoke and struggled to breathe. With his lungs burning from the fumes, he fought to pull himself away from the hot metal of the plane. Had they crashed?

A stab of pain ripped through his torso as a wave rushed over him, knocking him onto the deck of the ferry. Water crashed against the sides, spilling over onto the deck. People were panicking. They were sink-

ing. All these people surrounding him and there was no land in sight.

And Maddie... Where was Maddie? He tried to look around, but he couldn't get up. An orange flare arched through the air. He searched the hazy atmosphere. If she was here, he had to find her...

Grant woke with a start. He could feel the beads of sweat running down his forehead as he opened his eyes to bright fluorescent lights. Turning to his side, he groaned as another wave of intense pain racked his shoulder. His lungs struggled to draw in a breath, and he tried to stop the surge of panic that ensued.

Where was he?

He could only remember snippets of details. They'd been running from something...through the smoke... Maddie, Antonio, Ana... They needed to get to the taxi... to get away from...Reid.

"I was shot."

"It's about time you woke up. And yes, you took a bullet to the shoulder."

He hadn't even realized he'd spoken the words aloud until someone answered him. A blurry figure hovered over him. He forced his eyes to work together and bring the subject into focus, but the small act left him tired, so he closed his eyes.

After a moment, he opened them again. This time the looming figure was clearer. Black hair, neatly braided. Ebony skin. Blue-and-white uniform. "Where am I?"

"In a mission hospital a couple hundred miles north of the capital. You've been through surgery to have your shoulder repaired. You were lucky to have one of the best specialists around."

"What about…"

He wanted to say more, but his throat was so dry.

"Dr. Gilbert?" She handed him a glass of water.

"Yes." He took a sip and nodded. "Is she okay?"

"She's tired, but fine." The nurse checked the IV attached to his arm. "She's staying at the guesthouse that's connected with the hospital. I promised I'd call her as soon as you were awake."

Ten minutes later he watched Maddie sit down beside him and take his hand. She brushed back a strand of hair across his forehead and smiled.

"Hey, trooper. You've been through a lot. I'm glad to see you awake."

"You're okay?" His words came out choppy and horse, but he didn't care. He needed her to be okay.

"It's been a day I'd rather forget, but yeah… I'm okay."

She was so beautiful. Her dark hair was swept back in a ponytail. Dark brows framed gorgeous cinnamon eyes. But she looked tired. Lines had formed under her eyes, probably from lack of sleep. Details of the day were beginning to emerge. Today could have ended so different.

"The doctor's pleased with the surgery," she said. "You'll have a few weeks of PT ahead of you as soon as we can get you back to the States, but he expects a full recovery."

He made an attempt to lift his hand. Everything felt so heavy and the effort produced nothing.

"Still a bit numb?" she asked.

He nodded.

"That will pass. They've got you on some pain medicine as well. You can let them know if the pain gets to be too much."

"I'm okay for now," he said.

He could see the tears that had formed in the corners of her eyes. He wanted to kiss her. Take her in his arms and tell her that in spite of everything they'd gone through, everything was going to be okay. To tell her that once all of this was over, he still wanted that chance to get to know her better. And as soon as he had his strength back and could think clearly, they'd figure out how.

Maddie squeezed his hand, then pulled away. "You need to go back to sleep. Antonio and I are working to get us flights back to the States tomorrow. And you're going to need your strength."

He fought to keep his eyes open, knowing she was right, but there were things he needed to know. "What about Reid?"

She hesitated.

"Maddie?"

"No one knows where he is."

"Can he find us here?"

"Antonio and Colton don't think so, but I don't know. He's resourceful. But there is some good news. I called my mom and told her we were safe, and not ten minutes after I'd hung up, I received a call from the State Department," she began. "With the information we gave them, the US Drug Enforcement Agency—who apparently had already been working with officials from here—put together a sting operation. And while they still haven't found Reid, they did arrest the men he was working with, including one who was high up in the country's armed forces. They'll be tried in the region and hopefully be put away for a long, long time."

"That's good news."

"Yes, it is. They should be charged with everything from drug trafficking to the purchase of assault rifles, to surface-to-air missiles, to kidnapping. And I've been assured that our names have been cleared, and that we're safe now."

"Except for Reid. If he's still out there…"

"Any clout he had is gone, and he has to know that. Which means all of this should be over soon. Reid has nowhere to run."

He was relieved it was over, but there was something else he needed to know as well. "What about us?"

She pressed her lips together before answering. "I'll be honest, it scares me, Grant. I'm scared that things won't work out between us, and I'm scared that if they do, something will happen to you. Just like Darren, you haven't exactly chosen a low-risk career path. And everything that has happened over the past few days has only served as a reminder of that."

Was there really too much fear…too much of the past hanging over them to allow them a future together? He cleared his throat, knowing that right now wasn't the time to deal with that question, but neither was he willing to simply let the subject drop.

"Fear often holds too much power over us, doesn't it?" He spoke more to himself, than to Maddie, but she nodded in agreement.

And then there was the guilt… They were both powerful motivators. And far too often they'd tried to persuade him in the wrong direction.

"What if I said I'm falling in love with you?" He saw

the tears slipping down her cheeks as he spoke. For him, though, as he said it aloud, he knew it was true. "I've never met a woman who I was willing to fight for. Willing to find a way to make things work."

"I think you're wrong. It won't work between us, and I think deep down you know that as well." Her struggle showed in her eyes. "Today made everything seem so clear. Our lives are going in opposite directions. If I lose my heart to you, then lose you… I can't do that, Grant."

He ran his thumb across the back of her hand. That wasn't the answer he wanted to hear. "None of us know how long we have on this earth. You know that. I might die tonight, or I might live another fifty years."

"You should have been a lawyer."

He caught the smile that quivered on her lips as she spoke. "Let me in, Maddie. Give me a try. We'll never know what might happen if we stop now."

"I'm sorry, but I can't." She leaned over and kissed him on the cheek, her hair brushing against his face. "Good night, Grant."

He watched as she looked at him one last time, then turned around and walked out the door.

EIGHTEEN

Maddie stepped out into the garage, shivering at the drop in temperature from the house to where her stepfather was working. Two weeks had passed since she'd flown back to the States, and she still wasn't quite sure which way was up. She was almost ready to go back to work, but that feeling of incompleteness was back. Like she was missing something.

Part of her was still considering returning to Guinea-Bissau after the New Year. Because no matter what Reid had tried to do, her heart was still there with the women who needed her. Her work there left her feeling as if she was making a real difference. The other part of her, though, still felt bruised from the ordeal she'd gone through. And cautious of taking another risk.

"Aren't you freezing?" she asked, stopping next to the vintage mustang her stepfather was working on. "It can't be much more than thirty degrees in here."

He laughed. "Africa must have thinned your blood. Go stand by the portable heater over there, and you'll warm up quickly."

She zipped up her quilted jacket and dragged a metal stool in front of the heater. Warm air blew against her face. "Much better."

"To what do I owe the pleasure of a visit from my favorite daughter?"

Maddie smiled. He might be her stepfather, but he'd always loved her as if she'd been his own flesh and blood. "I just came by to grab one of Mom's cookbooks."

He glanced up at her. "You're cooking?"

"I'm baking a pie for tonight's Christmas Eve dinner. And don't sound so surprised."

He chuckled. "Oh, you've always been full of surprises." He chuckled again.

She breathed in the familiar scents of oil and gasoline she always associated with her stepfather when he was busy on a restoration project. Coming home had meant familiarity and family, and had helped balance out her unsettled emotions. But not completely. Not yet, anyway.

"I talked to my old boss today," she said. "I've decided to go back to work after the New Year, though it will be temporary. Just while Janet's on maternity leave."

"And after that?"

"I don't know."

"Your mother and I have been worried about you." Metal clanked against metal as he tightened a set of bolts on the fixer-upper parked in the middle of the garage. "You've just been so…quiet whenever you come by."

"Still tired, I guess. Adjusting to everything. The past few weeks have been…well, challenging to say the least."

"A week held hostage in an insurgent camp, a sinking

ferry, accused of drug trafficking…" he said. "I don't think 'challenging' is a strong enough description."

He was right.

She folded her hands in her lap and stared at a chipped nail. "I came out here to share some good news. I just received news on Reid Johnson."

"You did?" He stopped what he was doing and caught her gaze.

"He was arrested flying through South Africa on a fake passport, presumably on his way to South America."

"That's huge! I'd give you a hug, but I'm covered with oil."

She smiled. "It is big news. Even though I'd been assured he never made it back to the United States, I still feel like I can breathe again without constantly watching over my shoulder."

"I still can't believe you got caught up in that mess." He wiped his oily hands off on a rag. "At least it's over, and he can't come after you again."

Grant had been the one to call and tell her. Hearing his voice again had left her longing to see him. But he was back in Houston and she was here in Denver. She'd been right. Their lives were moving in opposite directions.

She picked at a loose thread on her jacket. "Can I ask you a question?"

He looked up at her. "Of course."

"How often do you think about Darren?"

"Not a day goes by when I don't think about him. He might have been my stepson, but his death left a huge void in my life that can't ever be replaced. Why?"

"I don't know. I've just been thinking about him a lot lately."

"Does this have anything to do with having been with Grant?"

"Grant?"

"He was best friends with your brother. You must have talked a lot about Darren."

"We did." She looked up, frowning, but felt her checks flush hearing his name. "But my question has nothing to do with Grant. I don't know. Maybe with all that's happened, along with the holidays, I'm just missing Darren more than normal."

Her stepfather folded his arms across his chest. "You know, your mother might claim that I'm not the most observant person, especially when it comes to things of the heart, but I have noticed there's something in your eyes when the subject of Grant is brought up. Have you talked to him since you flew home?"

"He's the one who called me today. We've exchanged a few emails. He's kept me up-to-date on what's happening with Reid and Ana. Do you remember the little girl I told you about?"

"Yes."

"Antonio found out her grandmother died six months ago. But he and his wife have taken her in."

"I'm happy for her," he said, "but you're changing the subject. You haven't told us a lot of the details of that trip, but I would assume it was pretty frightening and emotional for both of you."

What was she supposed to tell him? That Grant had kissed her and knocked her world on its edge? And that even though she knew her decision to walk away had been the right one, his face was the last thing she saw when she went to sleep at night and the first thing when she woke up?

"I guess what I'm saying," he continued, "is that I know you've been through a lot, but I'm here if you need me. For anything."

"Thank you." She stood up to bridge the gap between them and kissed him on the cheek. "I've got to run by the store and then make my pie."

"They sell frozen pies, you know."

"Funny. I'll see you tonight for dinner."

He picked up the wrench and walked back to the engine. "I'm glad you're home, Madison."

She smiled at him and then headed to the house, trying to push back the memory of Grant's kiss. Because whatever might have started on the other side of the Atlantic was over. Even if her heart still felt as if it had been shattered into a million pieces.

Three and a half hours later, Maddie studied the results of her attempts to make a homemade dessert. She'd made it through Anatomy and Biochemistry, but not Home Economics 101. But, glancing at the perfect photo of the pumpkin pie in her mom's recipe book and comparing it to her own creation she'd just pulled out of the oven, it was clear she'd missed something. Where the crimped edges hadn't burnt they'd flaked off, and while the picture boasted a creamy, caramel-colored filling, hers was a dull shade of orange.

Her father was right. She never should have volunteered to bring a dessert to her mother's Christmas Eve party that didn't come straight from the store. For some reason, she'd got it in her head that she wanted to make homemade holiday dessert from scratch like her mother always had. But instead of a meal straight from the pages of some glossy magazine, her attempts were more suited for a garbage disposal.

Maddie folded her arms across her chest debating whether or not she should simply toss the pie in the trash. The soothing voice of Michael Bublé filled the apartment with "All I Want for Christmas Is You." Grant's image filled her mind. Again, she pushed it away and eyed the pie again. Maybe she could cover it with a decorative mound of whipped cream. Surely it couldn't taste as bad as it looked.

The doorbell rang.

She glanced at the clock. She wasn't expecting anyone, and in fact she needed to leave for her parents' house within the next hour. Which meant she still needed to change into something a bit more festive than the jeans and T-shirt she was wearing...

The doorbell rang again.

She set down the pie and went to open the front door of her apartment.

There stood Grant, casually dressed in slacks, a smart-looking sweater and jacket, and a sheepish grin.

"Maddie... Hey... I was in the neighborhood."

"Grant?" She didn't try to hide her surprise as she hugged him, but then she pulled away as her heart suddenly took a nosedive. This had to be a dream. Grant Reese could not be standing at her front door. "I just spoke to you a few hours ago. I thought you were home in Houston."

"I was on my way home, actually, flying back from some meetings in Oklahoma City with a mine advisory group. I saw the flight to Denver on the board—"

"And you just decided to pop in unannounced." Her mind was still reeling.

His smile faded. "I'm sorry—"

"No, I'm sorry." She shook her head. "That came out all wrong, it's just that I don't know what to say."

"I tried to call."

"I left my phone in my bedroom."

"You look great."

"So do you." She tried to ignore the surge of emotions that swept through her. He'd lost some weight since he'd been shot, but even that hadn't erased his military physique. Give him a few more weeks, and she knew his daily trips to physical therapy would pay off. "How's your shoulder?"

"My physical therapist said that with a lot of hard work, I should be back to normal in a few weeks."

"I'm glad to hear that." Snow had begun to fall across her small front yard. "I'm sorry. You must be freezing. Come in, please. I'm still trying to wrap my mind around the fact that you're here."

He picked up a box from the wrought iron bench just outside her front door. "I brought you a pie."

Her eyes widened. "You brought me a pie?"

"Not just any pie. It's chocolate mint tart with ganache. You mentioned how much you wanted to eat one that day we were stuck on the ferry."

The day he'd kissed her.

She shoved away the thought. "You might have just come to my rescue again. I've been baking a pie for a Christmas Eve party at my parents' tonight." She glanced at the pie, and paused. "But I think you knew about that, didn't you? You talked to my mom."

"When I couldn't get ahold of you, I called your mom. She invited me to their party tonight, and when I asked what I could bring, she suggested your favorite pie. But I don't understand. If you made a pie…"

"There are still quite a few things you don't know about me."

Grant followed her through the living room of the apartment she'd sublet to a friend while she'd been away, and then stepped into the tiny kitchen.

"I have a confession. I'm a horrible cook." She picked up her pie and shot him a lopsided grin. "It's still a bit runny, burnt on the edges, crumbly…"

Grant grabbed a knife off the counter and proceeded to cut a sliver of the pie.

"What are you doing?"

"Sampling." He popped a bite into his mouth.

"It's awful, isn't it?"

He winked at her. "I'll give it a five and a half out of ten."

"Right." Maddie laughed at the ridiculous assessment. How was it that he could make her smile even in the worst circumstances? "You don't need to be so generous on my account. I think the fact that I will never be a chef has been made very clear today."

He popped another bite into his mouth. Obviously the man liked to torment himself. "Give me a few days with you in the kitchen, and I'll make you into cable television's next cooking sensation."

"I don't think so. This is the very reason why takeout was invented. For people like me, who can work wonders in the ER, but who will never turn out consistently decent meals." She eyed him suspiciously. "Besides, what are you? Some guru chef?"

"No, I just like to cook."

Another side of him she wanted to get to know. She stopped. No.

"Like, boxed macaroni and cheese or gnocchi and lasagna?" she asked instead.

He wiped the crumbs from his mouth with the back of his hand. "My specialty is the grill, but I can also whip up a fairly decent Italian meal."

She tugged nervously on the bottom of her T-shirt and laughed. Because staring into those stunning blue eyes only managed to reinforce the fact that she'd missed him. Way too much. And right now, in her tiny kitchen, he was close enough that she could almost feel his warm breath on her face as she inhaled the scent of his cologne.

He reached up and wiped his thumb across her cheek. "You had some…flour from baking."

She swallowed hard. Her heart refused to stop fluttering. He was so close she wanted to slip her arms around him and let him kiss her again, and for a moment, she thought that was exactly what he was going to do.

Instead, he took a step back, and she tried to fight the crazy disappointment. "Maddie?"

She blinked her eyes and looked up at him. "I'm sorry. I was just thinking."

He ran his hand down her sleeve. "About what?"

"About the last time I saw you." They'd flown home together the four thousand miles from Dakar to Washington, DC. The distance between them had felt even greater than their trip across the Atlantic.

He lowered his gaze. "The last time I saw you, you told me you were afraid of losing your heart. And if that's still how you feel, that's okay. But I needed to know for sure before I walk away for good."

Maddie swallowed hard, knowing that these were the words that had been hanging between them. And the questions she still had. She tried to form an answer, but wasn't sure what to say. What she did know was that she was getting tired of running. She'd run away when Darren died. Then run away from Ben. And now she'd run away from Grant.

She'd tried to find a way to keep her heart intact, and wasn't sure she was ready to break down the remaining wall left between them so she could face her fears head-on. Or if she even knew how. But she realized how much she'd missed him. And with him standing in front of her, she realized now how much she wanted him to stay.

Grant stopped himself from pulling her into his arms and kissing her. Instead, he tried to gauge her reaction to his showing up unannounced. His coming had been a crazy risk, and he knew it, but two weeks had passed and nothing he'd done had even begun to lessen the feelings he had for her. Talking to her on the phone today had triggered the impulsive decision to show up at her doorstep.

She was smiling, but still seemed as if she'd been caught off guard. Antonio's advice played through his mind. *It might be time for you to move on... Forgiveness is a choice... Sometimes you have to fight for a happy ending...*

Everything within him told him that Maddie Gilbert was worth pursuing.

"I know it was crazy to just show up, but…" He held up his hand, stopping short of reaching out and touching her. "I've missed you."

Grant hadn't intended his words to come out so blunt, but he also wasn't one to dance around the truth.

Maddie had sufficiently broken his heart once, and he wasn't keen on it happening again. In fact, if it weren't for the shooting that had literally grounded him these past couple weeks, he'd probably have been out chasing down some land mine and trying to forget Dr. Madison Gilbert instead of thinking constantly about her.

He could smell the subtle scent of her perfume. It engulfed him, drawing him to her like a magnet. He tried to read her expression, feeling that everything he was saying was coming out wrong. He wanted a soul mate. He wanted her. But that didn't change the fact that she had rejected him. And up to this point she'd given no indication that she wanted to reverse that decision.

"I'm sorry." He stumbled with his words. "I shouldn't have come."

"No. I'm glad you did. It's just that seeing you today caught me off guard."

There was a hint of sadness in her eyes as she looked up at him. She rested her hand briefly against his hand, her fingers burning a path across his skin. Once again, he stifled the urge to draw her into his arms and kiss her. But that was something he had no right to do.

Sometimes you have to fight to make things work.

Yet here he stood in front of her, breathing in her flower perfume and longing to reach out and touch her soft skin. In the tight confines of the kitchen, she was close enough to kiss, yet he didn't dare. Not until the two of them had a chance to talk. The few times they'd communicated over the past couple weeks had been nice, but he hadn't forgotten his need to know if there was any possibility that her heart had finally triumphed over the logical side of her mind.

She pulled a couple soft drinks out of the fridge and handed one to him before following him into the living room she'd decorated with a few colorful accents from Africa. He stopped in front of the small, lit Christmas tree on one of the end tables and sat down on the brown couch. She sat down in a chair across from him and pulled her legs up under her.

He leaned forward, suddenly uneasy. Funny how the chances of a land mine exploding in his face didn't scare him nearly as much as discussing matters of the heart. But it was time they laid everything out in the open between them. Only then would he be able to move forward. Whether or not it would be with Maddie, he still wasn't sure.

Grant popped open the tab and took a sip before balancing the can on his thigh with one hand.

"Can I ask you a question?" she asked.

"Of course."

For a full thirty seconds she stared at the blinking lights of the small Christmas tree perched in front of an open window. Traffic crossing the busy intersection outside shot by, mixed with the occasional sound of a blaring horn.

He waited.

"I know that in order to risk one's life for someone else there has to be a reason," she said finally. "Something that drives that person to put themselves in the line of fire day after day. Policeman and firemen. Soldiers, rescue workers, bodyguards…"

"And deminers," he finished for her.

She nodded. "Is Darren's death a motivating factor, or are there other reasons?"

He tried to avoid her gaze and looked instead at the

tree with its red and silver ornaments. "I've always felt that his death was my fault."

"Why?"

He wasn't sure why she wanted to know, but clearly it mattered to her. "Remember Camille?"

"Of course."

"When we graduated from high school, Darren's plans were to go to the local community college, marry Camille and take over her father's landscaping business. It was my idea to join the Marines. I talked him into it, figuring he could still return and have his life one day, but it would give us a chance to see the world before we settled down."

Her brow wrinkled as she looked at him. "You're wrong."

"What do you mean, I'm wrong?"

"While I have no doubt that he loved her, Darren had a lot of doubts about marrying Camille. He was only eighteen." She drew in a slow breath. "A couple years later, he told me that joining the military was the best decision he'd ever made. He felt like he was doing something great, like our father had. You gave him the courage to do that."

"Why didn't he ever tell me that?"

"I don't know." She shrugged. "Remember the recruiting letter that came in the mail your senior year?"

"Yes." That letter had been the catalyst that had gotten him thinking about the Marines in the first place.

"He was the one who went down to the recruiting office and used your name. He thought if the idea came from you instead of him, my mom might be more open to it. After losing our dad, he knew she wasn't going to like the possibility of him joining the armed forces. That she was afraid she'd lose him as well."

"He never told me any of this."

"The bottom line is that Darren went into the Marines because he wanted to serve his country. You have no reason to feel guilty over his death. He was proud of what he did, and in the end he was even willing to give his life for what he believed in. That's the one thing that has helped me be able to accept his death. I hope it helps you as well."

He nodded, knowing he still needed to process what she'd just told him but grateful for what she'd said.

She pressed her lips together and looked up to catch his gaze. "You're not the only one Darren's death has affected."

He sat quietly, waiting for her to continue.

"When you asked me why Ben and I broke up, I didn't tell you everything. I've realized these past couple weeks that I was afraid something might happen to him. Like my father when he died. And like Darren."

He listened, unsure of what to say other than that he was sorry.

"I never saw that I was slowly pulling myself away," she said. "I told myself it was because we were so different. That our goals in life simply didn't mesh. And while all of that was true, I now realize it was so much more than that."

"Are you telling me you're getting back together with Ben—"

"No… My relationship with Ben is completely over. We *were* headed in different directions, but I realized I was doing the same thing with you. Pushing you away because I didn't want to get hurt. I didn't want to be the one left behind."

She'd mentioned her fears. He wanted to understand more why she felt the way she did. "Tell me about your father. I know he died in a car wreck, but that's really all I know."

She ran her finger around the rim of her drink. "I was in the car with him the day he died. He'd taken me out to go horseback riding out in the country."

"How old were you?"

"Eight. On the way back into town, a drunk driver hit us on one of the windy roads. Killed my father instantly. The other driver was killed as well. I remember sitting on the side of the road waiting for someone to stop and help. Eventually a couple did and drove me to the hospital."

"Oh, Maddie." He caught the pain in her eyes, and with it the realization as to why she feared losing someone else close to her. He reached out and clasped her hands. "I can't even begin to imagine what you went through that day."

"I just… I wanted you to understand. That experience was what made me want to become a doctor. I wanted to be able to save lives." Still looking at the tree, she drew in a deep breath, then let it out slowly. "But I've also spent my whole life pushing people away, including God, at times. I've also realized that deciding not to run away, and actually following through, takes more courage than I ever imagined."

"Anything worth fighting for usually does," he said. He paused, not wanting to push her, but he needed to know how she felt. If she'd missed him as much as he'd missed her. If there was a chance for a relationship between them. "What about us? Are we worth fighting for?"

* * *

A slight smile played on Maddie's lips. Fear still lingered, but with it was something else. The remaining wall around her heart crumbled. He'd been right. There was no way to know the future, but she could grab on to today. And she wanted to. But this time with Grant at her side.

"I never thought I'd be saying this, but yes, we're worth fighting for."

"Yes?" Grant stood up and smiled. "Then I have a present for you."

"A present?" Maddie's eyes widened.

He pulled a small box out of his jacket pocket. "This is for you."

"I don't have anything—"

"There's only one thing I want from you this Christmas. And you've just given it to me."

Her heart fluttered as she pulled the wrapping off the present, her insides feeling as bubbly as every other child on Christmas Eve. Inside was a delicate silver bracelet.

"Grant, it's beautiful."

"Turn it over."

Inside had been engraved the words *Fearless Faith*.

He slipped it onto her wrist and kissed her hand. "I don't know what the future holds for us. But what I do believe without a doubt is that God brought together two people longing for the same thing. In finding forgiveness for myself, I found love."

Maddie's eyes brimmed with tears as she fingered the bracelet. "What were you going to do if things didn't turn out this way?"

"I don't know." His smile broadened. "Back in the

hospital, I told you I was falling in love with you. Nothing has changed. I decided that I wasn't ready to just give up on us."

"I…" The familiar footsteps of fear began creeping into the recesses of her heart. "I still have questions. What about your job? And mine? We don't even always live in the same country, and a long-distance relationship isn't something I—"

"I have a few job options that could bring me to Denver."

"You would do that? For me?" And, she realized she was willing to do the same for him.

He took her hands and nodded. "For us. Fearless faith, Maddie. That's what God calls us to." He squeezed her hands, and his touch began loosening the fear's rigid grasp. "If anyone's looked death in the face a thousand times it's me, but I won't allow my faith to waver anymore. And the same goes for our relationship."

Maddie smiled. "Sometimes you have to fight for a happy ending."

"Exactly." He ran his thumb across her cheek and kissed her slowly before pulling her against him. "And you're definitely someone worth fighting for."

* * * * *

Dear Reader,

I hope you enjoyed Grant and Maddie's story! A few weeks ago I visited an island off Africa's eastern coastline. There were stunning sunsets, boats bobbing on the water, open markets and palm trees waving in the breeze. While I was there, I have to be honest that I was very thankful I didn't experience any of the things Grant and Maddie went through.

And yet, I think most of us can relate to the issues of forgiveness they both faced. It really is true that "forgiveness is a choice." And not an easy one at that. In life we hurt people and people hurt us. We fall down and we have to get back up. We face heartache and disappointment and wish we could turn back the clock and start over.

It wasn't easy for Grant and Maddie to fight for their happy ending, just as it isn't easy for us. And while life can be challenging, my prayer is for each one of us to find that fearless faith that lets us step out and trust God to go before us!

Be blessed,

Lisa Harris

REQUEST YOUR FREE BOOKS!
2 FREE RIVETING INSPIRATIONAL NOVELS
PLUS 2 FREE MYSTERY GIFTS

Love Inspired®
SUSPENSE
RIVETING INSPIRATIONAL ROMANCE